"I'm sorry about earlier," Hannah said. "I shouldn't have run away."

"Interesting turn of phrase," Jeff replied.

"A trait I'm trying to change." Tonight, a part of her longed to embrace change.

"Let's eat." He drew her chair out, a gentlemanly gesture, then sat in the chair opposite her.

Hannah flushed. "You could have sat over here." She indicated the chair to her right.

He smiled. "If you'd prefer…"

"Not what I meant and you know it."

The smile deepened. "I'm good here for the moment. The extra space gives me a buffer zone."

This time Hannah smiled. His teasing look was tinged with a hint of compassion, just enough to help calm the encroaching waves within.

She wanted new memories. New chances. New beginnings. Isn't that why she'd come to Jamison in the first place?

You came here to hide. Nothing more, nothing less.

Then she wanted to stop hiding.

Books by Ruth Logan Herne

Love Inspired

Winter's End
Waiting Out the Storm
Made to Order Family
*Reunited Hearts
*Small-Town Hearts
*Mended Hearts

*Men of Allegany County

RUTH LOGAN HERNE

Born into poverty, Ruth puts great stock in one of her favorite Ben Franklinisms: "Having been poor is no shame. Being ashamed of it is." With God-given appreciation for the amazing opportunities abounding in our land, Ruth finds simple gifts in the everyday blessings of smudge-faced small children, bright flowers, fresh baked goods, good friends, family, puppies and higher education. She believes a good woman should never fear dirt, snakes or spiders, all of which like to infest her aged farmhouse, necessitating a good pair of tongs for extracting the snakes, a flat-bottomed shoe for the spiders, and the dirt…

Simply put, she's learned that some things aren't worth fretting about! If you laugh in the face of dust and love to talk about God, men, romance, great shoes and wonderful food, feel free to contact Ruth through her website at www.ruthloganherne.com.

Mended Hearts
Ruth Logan Herne

Love Inspired

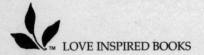

Recycling programs
for this product may
not exist in your area.

LOVE INSPIRED BOOKS

ISBN-13: 978-0-373-87696-9

MENDED HEARTS

Copyright © 2011 by Ruth M. Blodgett

www.LoveInspiredBooks.com

Printed in U.S.A.

Be still before the Lord and wait patiently for him; do not fret when men succeed in their ways, when they carry out their wicked schemes. Refrain from anger and turn from wrath; do not fret—it leads only to evil. For evil men will be cut off, but those who hope in the Lord will inherit the land.
—*Psalms* 37:7–9

Dedication

This book is dedicated to Melissa Endlich, whose patience and rolling pin have proven necessary on more than one occasion. Your continued confidence blesses me abundantly.

And to Amanda, Seth, Lacey and Karen, four wonderful high school teachers who've worked the front lines of adolescent development. God bless you guys!

Acknowledgments

Wonderful teachers are never forgotten.
Special thanks to Mrs. Fenlon (now Mrs. Steiner),
Sr. Mary Cordis, Sr. Mariel (deceased), Sr. Natalia,
Mrs. Bagley and Thomas Dowd. I'm grateful for your encouragement and kindness. And to Alice McCarthy,
my Girl Scout leader, who became a stand-in at every parental function. Alice, thank you for treating an abnormal situation with sweet normalcy. God blessed you with a generous heart and I thank you for the times you sat with me, accompanied me and covered my "dues."
There's a special place in heaven for people like you.

Special thanks to Mandy for traipsing the hills of Allegany with me, taking the time to meet perfect strangers with a smile and a handshake. Weren't those sheriffs adorable???
To Beth and Jon for their constant help in so many ways.
To Matt and Karen and Seth and Lacey for their continued support and help. And to Zach and Luke who advise from afar and take the couch so I can have the bed when I visit them. You guys rock.

To the Seekers, www.seekerville.blogspot.com.
Your light shines for so many. I'm blessed to have you in my life. Audra, thanks for the read. You rock. Andrea, for the steady belief for so many years.

And especially to Dave for his continued love and support. He makes a mean tuna fish sandwich! Love you, Dude.

Prologue

Jeff Brennan stood slowly, facing his illegitimate half brother, their gazes locked, a silent war of wills waging in their squared-off stature. Nice to see that twenty years of separation had changed absolutely nothing. "What do you want, Matt? What are you doing here?"

Matt Cavanaugh didn't match Jeff's caustic tone, but then he'd always had a way of wriggling out of things right up until he nearly cost Katie Bascomb her life. He did cost her a leg, but guys like Matt didn't worry about things like consequences. Ever.

Matt leveled a firm look at Jeff, not cringing. Not asking forgiveness. Not apologizing for all he'd put the family through two decades back. Which meant he might need to be punched. And with the current demands and conditions of Jeff's job as the chief design engineer for Walker Electronics, his business partner Trent Michaels called away for life-threatening family illness and the in-house rush to nail down a mobile surveillance system designed to keep an eye on threatened American borders, Jeff was ready to duke it out with just about anyone.

Throw in the matching funds library project his grandmother and CEO threw at him an hour ago, and Matt had no idea how close he was to risking his life.

Jeff swallowed a growl, glanced down, then up. The look in Matt's eyes said he might just be getting it, but on an already bad day, the last thing Jeff wanted or needed was the long-awaited showdown with his lawbreaking half brother. "I said, what do you want?"

Matt raised his hands in a conciliatory gesture. "I'm in town to scout out some possible work. I'm a housing contractor now, and I didn't want to blindside you or anyone else in the family by running into you in the street."

"You've grown a conscience?" Jeff's hands tightened. His skin prickled. The hairs on the nape of his neck rose in quiet protest. "Since when?"

Matt didn't answer the question. "I've come to make amends, Jeff."

"Too little, too late."

A tiny muscle in Matt's jaw tightened. "You could be right. I hope you're wrong. But I wanted to come here and see you face-to-face. Pave the way."

"So you're in town looking for work." Jeff mused over the words, wishing Matt wasn't so calm while he felt ready to jump the desk and settle old wrongs. "Or you're here because Walker Electronics is doing better and you want a piece of the pie."

Matt swiped Jeff's office a quick glance. "Right. I just now decided to fulfill a lifelong yearning to understand microchips, nanoseconds and satellite-fed communications. Sorry, but that part of our father didn't bleed through to me."

"No." Jeff shut his desk drawer with more force than necessary. "You got the drinking, gambling, womanizing and lawbreaking genes. How's that working for you, Matt?"

Matt stepped back. "I didn't come to fight, Jeff. I just wanted you aware. And if you'll point me toward Helen's office, I'll let her know, as well."

What Jeff wanted was to show Matt the exit in no uncertain terms, but that would label him an even bigger jerk. He hiked a thumb left. "Out the door. Down the hall. I know she's there because we just finished a meeting about a matching fund drive for the Jamison library."

"Your grandfather's wishes."

"Yes."

Matt nodded and backed toward the door. "I'm not looking to get in your way down here."

"You already did."

Matt acknowledged that with a shrug and a straight-on look. "Those are your issues, then."

He turned, leaving Jeff with nothing but riled-up memories, twenty years of absence not enough to warrant Matt's presence as a welcome addition.

His grandmother would disagree. Jeff knew that. She'd always seen Matt as a broken soul, a lost kid, a troubled heart.

Whereas Jeff saw a conscienceless user, just like their father.

Long ago, Peter had asked the Lord about forgiving his brother, wondering if seven times was enough. And Jesus said no. Not nearly enough. Which only meant Jeff had some serious work to do if forgiving Matt was added to his already overflowing plate.

Chapter One

Megan Romesser's eyes brightened as Hannah Moore walked through the back door of Grandma Mary's Candies on this quiet September afternoon. Quiet equated good in Hannah's book, because she longed to vent loud and long, knowing Megan would listen, commiserate and then tell her to get on with it.

Megan understood the role of a good friend.

But venting would mean explaining why heading up a library fundraising drive with weekly meetings and full immersion into what everyone else considered normal life thrust Hannah into an emotional tailspin. Opening that door meant facing things she'd tucked aside years ago.

If not now, when?

How about never?

Hannah shoved the internal questions aside. If keeping that door closed guarded her mental health, then so be it.

She nodded toward the trays of fresh candy and the wall of boxed chocolates shipped in from Grandma Mary's Buffalo-based factory. "Just being around this much chocolate adds inches to my hips. Why do I work here? To torture myself?"

"To see me." Megan sent her a quick grin, finished packing an order, then waved toward the back. "New sponge candy in the minikitchen. See what you think."

"I love the perks of this job. Have I mentioned that lately?"

"Which is why you run voraciously. Nothing sticks on you."

"A blessing and a curse."

"Ha." Megan sent a doubtful look over her shoulder. "Not packing on pounds is never a curse. Bite your tongue."

"Let's just say I'm not afraid to augment as needed," Hannah shot back, grinning. "Aiding and abetting my lack of curves."

Megan laughed out loud. "Seriously, Hannah, the way you look in a dress? In your running gear? Head-turning. Brat."

"Thanks." Hannah nipped a piece of fresh sponge candy, closed her eyes in appreciation and breathed deep. "Wonderful. Marvelous. Words escape me."

"That'll do for the moment. The chocolate is smooth enough?"

"Like silk."

"Sweet enough?"

"The perfect blend of slightly bitter chocolate to golden, sugary honeycomb. Need any more convincing?"

"I could use you to write my ad copy." Megan grinned, then turned to answer the wall phone. "Grandma Mary's Candies, Megan speaking. Hey, darlin', when are you coming home?"

Honeymooner talk. Hannah moved into the kitchen, removing herself from the inevitable love-yous and miss-yous of being separated for two whole days.

Right now, the last thing Hannah needed was another reminder of her empty life.

She tried to appear normal. She'd done a morning stint at the library, followed by a mandatory meeting with Helen Walker, CEO of Walker Electronics, which put her into this current tizzy. Now she would put in four hours of work helping Megan in the family candy store in Wellsville.

Working odd jobs offered a semblance of normal, but normal had disappeared on a rainy afternoon almost five years ago, taking a hefty part of her self-reliance with it.

Pretense worked now. Fake it till you make it, an old sales adage that applied. Only Hannah hadn't gotten to the "make it" part yet. Lately she'd been wondering if she ever would. Perhaps Helen Walker had been right, maybe shouldering this library fundraising task would be good for her. Anything that pushed her out of her self-imposed comfort zone wasn't bad, right?

Depends on your definition of bad, her inner voice scoffed.

Oh, she knew bad. Been there, done that, had no desire to return. Not ever again. Keeping her responsibilities minimal meant downsizing risk, and that had become her current mantra.

"Hannah?"

"Yes?" She poked her head around the corner, then shifted her attention to the phone. "You done with lover boy?"

Megan laughed. "Yes, but he's not coming home until tomorrow. Problems with staffing at the Baltimore store. Wanna do a movie tonight?"

Hannah shook her head. "Too nice to stay inside. What about walking the ridge?"

"As in *walk,* not run?"

Hannah smiled as she weighed sponge candy into one-pound boxes. "Promise."

"I'm in. You're okay on your own here?"

Hannah glanced around the empty store. "Fine. You're leaving?"

"Just for a bit. Ben needs a ride home from the restaurant."

Ben was Megan's developmentally challenged younger brother who lived in a group home a few blocks from the store. "You go get Ben. I'll do quality control on the sponge candy. And maybe the caramels, as well."

"Can't be too careful." Megan paused and gave Hannah a quick hug on her way out. "Are you okay?"

"Fine. Why?" Steadying her features, Hannah glanced up.

"You seem a little off."

"I'm a girl. That happens, doesn't it?"

"Hmm." Megan didn't look convinced. "If you need to talk…"

"Which I don't."

"Even so." Megan gave Hannah a look, her expression unsure. "If you do, I'm available."

"I know." Hannah turned her attention back to the task at hand, shoulders back, feet firm. "I appreciate it."

"Well, then." Megan sounded dubious but she'd never delve. More than Hannah's friendship, she respected her right to privacy, a wonderful plus in this age of girlfriends-know-all.

Hannah couldn't afford to have anyone know all. Bad enough she carried that burden on her shoulders. She refused to bring others down. But that weighted the yoke, and with the Allegheny foothills hinting gold and red, fall's beauty carried heavy reminders of love and loss.

The antique bell announcing a customer's arrival provided a welcome interruption. Hannah left the half-filled box on the scale and moved to the front of the east-facing store. A man stood scanning a new display kiosk, a man who'd become distressingly familiar two hours ago. "May I help you?"

Surprise painted his features as Jeff Brennan turned from a corner display. Hannah fought the rise of emotions his expression inspired. In three years she hadn't crossed paths with this man, and now twice in one day?

Obviously God had a sense of humor, because the last person Hannah wanted to be around was a rising young executive, no matter how great he looked in gray tweed, the steel-and-rose pinstriped tie a perfect complement to the silver-toned oxford. She'd seen enough in the library council meeting to know he was self-confident, self-assured and slightly impatient, a condition that might arise from lack of time or lack of compassion, not that she cared.

His crisp, clean, business-first air had Brian's name written all over it, a CEO in the making, driven and forward-thinking. With the leaves beginning their annual dance of color, thoughts of her former fiancé only worsened matters. She shoved the memories aside, kept her expression calm and stepped forward, determined to get through this library fundraiser somehow, since her library contract allowed her no other choice.

"You've got time to work here, but you're reluctant to help with the new library?" The hint of resentment in Jeff's tone said her lack of enthusiasm was unappreciated in light of Helen and Jonas Walker's sacrifices.

But then Jeff had no idea what dragons loomed in her past as summer faded to fall and kids marched off to school, pencils sharp, their backpacks fresh and new, a world she'd been part of until that dark November day.

She met his gaze, refusing to let the clipped tone get to her. "My library job in Jamison is part-time. Last I looked life was full-time and that includes living expenses. An extra job helps pay the bills since the county couldn't afford more hours in the library budget."

"And you tutor?"

He'd actually been listening when she'd tried to beg off the fundraising committee earlier, but that shouldn't surprise her. You didn't get to Jeff Brennan's rung on the corporate ladder at thirty-plus without having a working brain. Of course being the boss's grandson couldn't hurt, but somehow she didn't see that happening at Walker Electronics. She slipped on fresh plastic gloves, ignored his question and indicated the glass-fronted candy display with a tilt of her head. "Would you like a hand-chosen collection, Mr. Brennan?"

His eyes narrowed, his look appraising once again. She got the idea that Jeff Brennan did a lot of appraising.

Well, he could stuff his appraisals for all she cared.

Feigning patience she waited, a box in hand, letting him make the next move. Which he did.

"Are you free for dinner tomorrow night?"

It took her a moment to register the words, shield her surprise, think of a response and then shelve the comeback as rude, a quality she chose not to embrace.

This is not Brian.

And yet the quick looks, the straight-on focus, the let's-get-down-to-business mode pushed too many buttons at once, especially with the distant hills hinting gold behind him.

He angled his head, his eyes brightened by her reaction. Which was really a nonreaction, and he seemed to find that almost amusing.

Dolt.

"I'm not, no."

"Wednesday?"

"The library is open until eight on Wednesday."

He sent her an exaggerated look of puzzlement, crinkled his eyes and moved closer, his manner inviting. "You can't eat after eight o'clock? Are you like one of those little aliens that couldn't eat after midnight?"

"Thanks for the compliment. Sorry. Busy."

"Look, Miss Moore…"

"Hannah."

A smile softened his features; he was probably remembering they'd had this conversation before, like two hours ago in the conference room of Walker Electronics.

"Hannah. Pretty name. It means favored. Or favored grace."

"And you know this because?"

"I looked it up on my computer when I got back to my office."

Add *smooth* to the list of reasons to avoid Jeff Brennan. Too smooth, too handsome, too winsome with his short curly brown hair, hazel eyes, strong chin, great nose and lashes that girls spent way too much money for.

Hannah flashed him a cool smile, not wanting or needing to dredge up a past best left buried, not this time of year. "You and the wife picking baby names, Mr. Brennan?"

He raised unfettered hands. "Not married, never have been, nor engaged. And dinner is simply so you and I can go into Thursday's meeting on the same page with similar goals, if neither one of us successfully ducks this project. No strings, no ties, no ulterior motives."

The sensibility of his argument enticed Hannah to accept. Chronic fear pushed her to refuse. She waffled, hating this indecision, longing to be the person she used to be. Strong. Self-motivated. Forceful.

But that was before Ironwood, and nothing had been the same since. She shook her head, needing to decline and hating the cowardice pushing the emotion. "I can't. Sorry."

He'd tempted her.

Good.

She'd telegraphed the reaction as she weighed her response, a quick, vivid light in her eyes, quenched as seconds ticked by. Jeff liked the bright look better, but either way, something about Hannah Moore piqued his interest.

Which made no sense because shy, retiring women weren't his type, although something in her stance and bearing made him think she wasn't as timid as she made out. Perhaps hesitant was a better word, and that only made him wonder what caused the timorous look behind those stunning blue eyes.

And if he couldn't persuade Grandma that his sister Meredith was the better choice to cochair these weekly meetings, he had to establish a common ground with this woman. Clearly she shared his displeasure about spending the better part of a year on the project.

Even with her long blond hair pulled back in a ponytail for her candy store stint, she was lovely. And cautious, a trait he'd learned to deal with if not love because his mother embraced caution as her middle name. But beneath the carefully constructed and controlled features, he sensed something else.

Right now he needed a cooperative attitude with this whole library business, and since he'd happened upon her here, at the Romesser family's new tribute store, fate was obviously throwing her into his path. Or maybe it was the fact that he needed a box of chocolates for a friend's wife who'd just given birth. Either way, Jeff wasn't about to waste an opportunity. He shifted his attention to the chocolates. "I need a pound and a half of mixed chocolates including cherry cordials, if you don't mind."

Her face softened, dissipating the glimpse of worry. "Josie O'Meara."

He laughed, amazed. "How'd you know?"

Hannah leaned forward as if sharing a secret. "She stopped by for one cherry cordial nearly every day until she delivered. It was her way of rewarding herself for being a working mom with a baby on board."

"That's Josie, all right. Do you know all your customers like that? At the library and here? And the kids you tutor?"

She shook her head as she filled the box, then shrugged. "Yes and no. It's easy because I work at small venues. If they were bigger, it might not be the same."

Somehow Jeff doubted that. Hannah's soul-searching eyes said she was a woman of marked intelligence.

So why was she working part-time in an out-of-the-way postage-stamp-size library, gilding the lack of pay by boxing chocolates?

She wrapped the box in paper decorated with tiny dinosaurs, perfect for the mother of a brand-new baby boy. "Tell her I packed extra cherry cordials in there from me. And that Samuel is a great name."

"Samuel was Hannah's son in the Bible, wasn't he?"

Her eyes shadowed, the hint of self-protection reemerging.

"That will be eighteen dollars, please."

"Of course." He let the subject slide, not sure how or why, but pretty certain he'd prickled a wound. "And Wednesday night?"

She glanced away, then down.

"I can pick you up or we can meet at The Edge."

He waited, counting the ticks of the clock, then leaned forward. "And can you wear something that doesn't remind me of how pretty your eyes are? That doesn't augment that shade of blue?"

She jerked up, the shadow chased away by annoyance. "Maybe. Maybe not. I'll meet you there. Eight-thirty."

"Perfect." He raised up the signature green-and-tan striped paper bag bearing Grandma Mary's logo. "See you then. And thanks for the candy."

He felt her gaze on him as he left the store, the bell jangling his departure. He headed left toward the hospital, but refused to glance back to see if she watched him stroll down the sidewalk.

Nope.

Let her wonder if he'd totally forgotten her the minute he stepped through the door, which he hadn't. Give her something to stew over instead of whatever shadowed her expression.

Although he did understand the concept of shouldering burdens firsthand. His father's illicit drug and gambling habits turned Neal Brennan's brilliant mind into a disaster, nearly toppling their family business. Jeff intended to do whatever it took to polish the Brennan name until it gleamed.

Matt Cavanaugh's sudden reappearance in the area didn't make his goal easier, but Jeff refused to dwell on that new twist. He'd meet with Grandma later, get her opinion. And he'd run an internet check on his half brother, see what he could find. Good or bad, he'd face any showdowns with Matt well-informed.

And Hannah…

Hopefully he could establish ground rules with her over supper. If they were on the same page, perhaps they could jump-start the library fundraiser quickly. Start-up was always the most time-consuming part of fundraising. Between his grandparents' and mother's philanthropy, Jeff had seen that firsthand. So he'd get together with Hannah, make a plan and set it in motion. And the whole dinner with a beautiful woman thing?

Not too shabby either.

Chapter Two

"**D**inner with Jeff Brennan? At The Edge? Oh, girlfriend, you are travelin' with the big guns now." Megan nudged Hannah as they crested the hill at the edge of town, late-day shadows beginning to lengthen.

"Stop." Hannah scowled and increased the pace of the walk deliberately. Maybe if Megan was winded, she couldn't ask questions.

"Have you met before?"

Not winded enough. "No."

"Ever?"

"No. And don't look at me that way. I've only been here a few years."

"But he's everywhere. Does everything. And not only because his family is like the royal family of Allegany County, but because he's a people person. Jeff loves to be in the thick of things. A born manager."

The last thing Hannah wanted was to be managed. "Whereas I prefer the background, thanks."

Megan frowned, hesitated, then waded in. "You're great with people, Hannah."

"I've got nothing against people. I just don't like getting involved."

"But—"

"And I'm busy."

"Do you need me to cut your hours at the store? Would that help?"

"Not if I want to continue to pay my bills." Hannah started to surge ahead, then came to a complete stop, aggravated, wishing she didn't have to explain herself. Explaining meant she might slip back into the dark waters of things she avoided. "See, that's the thing. I love working at the library because it's small. Quiet. I help a few people here and there. It's perfect for me. If we make it all big and beautiful, I'll be expected to do all kinds of things, all the time. I like things the way they are, Meg."

"Why is bigger bad?" Megan wondered. "I would think you'd embrace the idea of helping more kids, more families, providing more books, more chances."

Megan's words struck deep.

Hannah had provided a lot of chances for kids back in the day. She'd gone out on limbs, taken the bull by the horns, encouraging, offering young adults a rare experience. She'd been a risk taker then, in her beautifully equipped classroom, before life flipped upside down.

She was a rabbit now. Emotional necessity ruled the cautious lifestyle she'd adopted. It suited her duck-and-cover personality.

"I'll be on the committee if you'd like," Megan offered. "Would that help? Then we could strategize while we're at the store together. Kill two birds with one stone."

"What horrible bird hater thought up that analogy?"

Megan laughed. "Don't change the subject. What are you wearing Wednesday night?"

"Nothing special."

"What about my blue sarong? The one I brought back from Hawaii?"

"Hmm. Show up at the library in a sarong. Perfect for

children's hour." She flashed Meg a wry look. "End of story. And this discussion. Besides, I can't wear blue."

"What? Why?"

Hannah felt a blush rise from her neck and resented her fair complexion for the first time in several years. "We need another color."

"You've lost me."

Hannah sighed. "He said if I wear blue he'll have a hard time concentrating on anything besides my eyes."

Megan ground to a halt, pebbled stones skittering beneath her feet. "He said that? Out loud?"

Hannah stopped, as well, directed a bemused look to her friend and sighed. "He did, but it was most likely to throw me off track because he wants this project done. If he can't weasel his way out of it and pawn it off on his sister."

"Meredith's back?"

"If that's his sister's name, then yes."

"Huh." Megan frowned and resumed walking. "I'll have to call her, see what's up. You'll love her. She's funny and down-to-earth. And she does great hair and nails."

"Corporate boy's sister is a hairdresser? Why did I not see that coming?"

"She loves it. And she's wonderful, like I said. The Walkers aren't your typical rich family."

Jeff Brennan had seemed pretty typical earlier that day. Focused, frenetic and finite, a path she'd traveled once before. No way was she going down that road again.

"Is there such a thing as typical rich anymore?" Hannah asked. "There's some pretty weird millionaires running around these days."

"And some downright nice ones."

Hannah laughed. "Present company excluded, of course. Although I hear candy-store entrepreneurs maintain their delightful normalcy because of their choice in wives."

"Makes sense to me." Megan offered agreement with an

elbow nudge to Hannah's arm. "And wear the blue. Call his bluff."

A part of Hannah wanted to do just that.

Another part couldn't take the risk.

The gold top Hannah wore said she had no intention of jumping into the water with him, metaphorically speaking. The fact that the soft knit looked just as good as the blue simply brightened Jeff's evening.

Watching as she wove her way through the tables of The Edge's second dining room Wednesday evening, it was impossible to miss the strength of her moves, athletic and lithe.

That inborn agility appeared out of step with her other body language. Her careful facial movements belied by nervous hands and the inward expression that shadowed her eyes intermittently.

Edgy hands. Cloaked expression. A rough combination, all told, reminiscent of his mother in the bad days of his parents' publicly awful marriage.

He stood as she approached the table. The hostess smiled as she indicated a chair. Jeff pulled the chair out for Hannah, waited until she was comfortably seated, then sat in the adjacent chair.

"You had to choose that one, didn't you?" She met his gaze with a quiet look of challenge. "Being across from me wasn't close enough? Or intimidating enough?"

"I intimidate you?" Jeff unfolded his napkin, brow drawn, but not too much, just enough to let her know he could quirk a grin quickly. "Thanks, I'll remember that."

"Annoyed, possibly," she corrected, looking more sure of herself. "Intimidated? No."

"Good to know, although I was starting to feel pretty good about myself. I've been trying to intimidate my sister for years. No go."

"And yet still you try."

He grinned agreeably. "A brother's job. Would you like an appetizer, Hannah? The Edge has great stuffed mushrooms. And the owner makes Shrimp le Rocco, huge shrimp done in a wine and cream sauce with a hint of Cajun, just enough to give it life."

"Are you auditioning for the Food Network?"

"I'm a Paula Deen guy," he admitted, smiling. "All that butter. Cream. Southern drawl. And she's sweet but tough. Reminds me of Grandma."

"Your grandmother is one strong lady." Hannah looked more at ease talking about Grandma. She settled back in her seat and fingered her water glass, then smiled and nodded at the waitress as they gave their drink and appetizer orders.

The smile undid him, just a little. Sweet. Broad. Inviting. She had a generous mouth when it wasn't pinched in worry.

"She is." Jeff settled back, as well, surveyed her and sighed openly. "Which means you're stuck with me, I'm afraid. My attempts to get Meredith on board fell on deaf ears. Seems she's got other fish to fry."

"Aha."

"And your attempts? Still unsuccessful?"

She shrugged. "I didn't try. There's a part of me..." She paused, shifted her attention, then drew it back to him, reluctant. "That thinks this will be good for me."

Good for her?

Jeff considered the words, the look, then chose not to probe. Seeing fundraising as therapeutic was beyond his understanding, but if they both had to be involved, at least they'd both accepted the fact.

Grudgingly.

However, sitting with her, watching her, eyeing the lights and shadows that played across her face, candlelight mixed with emotion, he didn't feel all that grudging. He felt...

Drawn.

But he couldn't be for two reasons: women of indecision

annoyed him, which was precisely why he got on so well with his grandmother, and he had no time to devote to thoughts of a relationship.

If not now, when?

Jeff shut down the annoying mental reminder, thoughts of microchips, rare metal glazings and mobile communications taking precedence for the foreseeable future.

His grandmother was a thinker, doer and planner. Jeff followed her lead. Plan your work, then work your plan. He'd constructed his life that way, a goal setter to the max, doing anything to eliminate similarities to his narcissistic father. His appearance and affinity for inventive science labeled him as Neal Brennan's son, but that was as far as the resemblance went.

Jeff pushed himself to be better. Stronger. Wiser. Although lately a part of him felt worn by having to be on the cutting edge constantly, he couldn't afford the appearance of weakness. Not now. Not ever.

He leaned forward, elbows braced, hands locked, noticing how the freckles dusting her cheeks blended with her sunkissed skin. "Hannah."

She noted his shift and a hint of amusement sparked in her eyes, a look that downplayed her nervous gestures. "Yes, Jeff?"

She was playing him in her own way. He leaned closer. "Since we're stuck with each other…"

"At weekly meetings." She drawled the words, her tone teasing.

He sighed, then nodded as if pained. "For the better part of a year until enough money is raised."

She met his look, but that small spark of humor in her eyes kept him moving forward. "Might I suggest we come to a mutual agreement?"

"That you buy me supper once a week? That sure would help my grocery budget."

He grinned without meaning to. "We'll put that on the negotiating table. Does that mean you'd cook for me once a week?"

"No."

"Obviously we need to work on your bargaining skills. You never say no right out. It puts the other players off."

"What if I'm not into games?" she asked. She eyed her water glass, then him. "Game playing isn't my thing."

"When it comes to raising funds, we're all into games," he assured her.

She sat back purposely.

"And when we're talking cajoling benefactors, you and I will need to be on the same page," he continued. "Which means we stay open to any and all ideas as if they're workable, even if we know they're not."

"We lie."

He shook his head. "Not lie. Improvise."

"Lead people on."

"Not in a bad way." He studied her, and knit his brow, wondering. "As chairpeople, you and I need to appear open to others' ideas even if we've already planned a course of action."

"What if their ideas have merit?"

"We incorporate them, of course. But only if they don't take us off track."

His words quenched the spark of amusement in her eyes. "So as long as it's your way, it's a go."

"No, not really."

"That's what you said."

"What I said was spawned by your refusal to cook for me," he shot back, hoping humor would soften the moment, noting her withdrawal with a glance. "You said no too quickly. If you'd said 'I'll consider that and get back to you,' at least then I'd feel like I have a chance. And that's how contributors want to feel. Like they're appreciated. Considered."

"So because I shot down your plea for a home-cooked meal, I'm being lectured on the ins and outs of fundraising?"

He sat back, confused. "Listen, I—"

She slid forward in her seat as if ready to do battle, a tactical move that surprised him considering her previous timidity. "For your information, I am perfectly capable of running this thing completely on my own. So feel free to take yourself back to Grandma and tell her I can fly solo, because it will be way more fun than dealing with a corporate know-it-all who pretends other people's opinions matter when clearly they don't." She stood, back straight, face set, determination darkening her blue eyes. "And as for cooking you dinner, not only would you be wise to not hold your breath, you might want to consider a weekly grocery delivery service so the inconvenience of shopping doesn't interrupt your goals and ambitions. Why should something as mundane as food interfere with total world domination? Let your grandmother know I'll be glad to take this on independently. End of discussion."

She strode out of the restaurant, shoulders back, head high, not glancing left or right.

Total world domination? Jeff sat back, mystified. Her reaction revealing two things. She had plenty of backbone, a trait he'd respect more when he wasn't being publically reamed out over nothing.

And someone had done quite a number on her and he was paying the price.

He refused to glance around, not caring to see the surprise or sympathy the other diners might bestow his way.

The waitress appeared looking slightly stressed. "Uh-oh."

"Yeah." He sent her a look of bemusement. "Can I have the appetizers to go, please? Looks like I'm dining on my own tonight."

"Of course. I'll be right back."

Her look of sympathy didn't help his deflated ego.

Smacked down in public.

Ouch.

That hadn't happened in…ever. Which made it almost interesting, despite the embarrassment factor.

Still…she hadn't looked faint or weak or intimidated as she headed out that door after dressing him down. She'd looked strong. Angry. Invigorated.

Not exactly the emotions he'd been going for, but at least they were normal. Understandable. He glanced at his watch, nodded his thanks to the young waitress and tried to exit with his head high, fairly sure half the dining room was just too polite to stare.

They didn't need to. He felt conspicuous enough as it was.

Chapter Three

She'd call Helen first thing tomorrow, Hannah decided as she kicked off her shoes in her apartment fifteen minutes later. If she had to embrace this task, she'd take the helm and do it alone. The idea of dealing with a power-hungry ladder climber like Jeff Brennan touched too many old chords. Her teaching success. Brian's drive and goal-setting passions. The perfect couple when all was well.

No, being around Jeff nudged too many insecurities to the surface. She was better, she knew that.

But still scared. And scarred. Emotionally, if not physically.

The doorbell rang.

Hannah headed to the front entry, surprised. She stopped as her heart shifted somewhere closer to her gut.

Jeff stood framed in the glass, a to-go sack in his hand, his expression sincere, almost as if he was truly sorry for setting her off when he'd done nothing wrong except evoke bad memories.

Self-recriminations assaulted her from within. She opened the door, and sighed, letting the door's edge offer support. "I shouldn't have walked out on you like that."

"Why did you?"

Hannah refused to open that box, although lately the cover seemed determined to inch off on its own, a concept that both worried and strengthened her. "You struck a nerve."

"Sorry." He didn't demand an explanation, just stood there looking truly apologetic. He hoisted the bag. "I can't eat these alone. I know you're hungry, and I don't want to start off on the wrong foot."

The gentility behind this surprise move softened her heart. Meg had proclaimed Jeff to be a downright nice guy, invested in the community. At this moment, Hannah couldn't disagree. "Come in."

He smiled, not triumphant or teasing, but amiable and friendly as if he'd teased her enough for one night. A part of her wished she could play those getting-to-know-you games she used to be good at, but she'd lost that skill and had no interest in resurrecting it.

Get it back.

She sensed the inner admonition, felt the internal thrust forward and resisted, her fear of risk standing its ground.

"Do not be afraid for I am with you...."

Isaiah's words tinkered with her heart, her soul.

"I will strengthen you and help you...."

"This is nice, Hannah." Jeff swept the front room an approving look, then raised the bag again. "Here or in the kitchen?"

"The kitchen's fine."

"Lead the way." He followed her, set the bag on the table, then faced her.

"I'm sorry about earlier. I shouldn't have run away."

"Interesting turn of phrase."

She grimaced acceptance. "A trait I'm trying to change." Tonight, with him here, delicious smells wafting from the to-go containers, a part of her longed to embrace change. And food. "I'll get some plates."

"Perfect."

It wasn't perfect, she knew that, but by coming here he'd leveled their playing field. Brian would never have swallowed his pride and come calling to make amends. She withdrew two plates from the cupboard and turned to find Jeff procuring silverware from the drawer alongside the sink.

"These okay?" He held up two knives and two forks.

She nodded. "Fine, yes."

"Then let's eat." He drew her chair out, a gentlemanly gesture, then sat in the chair opposite her.

Hannah flushed. "You didn't have to do that."

"What?" He looked genuinely puzzled about her meaning.

"Sit over there. Here would have been fine." She indicated the chair to her right with a nod.

He raised a brow in amusement. "If you'd prefer…"

"Not what I meant and you know it."

The smile deepened. "I'm good here for the moment. The extra space gives me a buffer zone."

This time Hannah smiled. His banter was tinged with a hint of compassion, just enough to help calm the encroaching waves within. Her therapist had told her she'd know when to test the waters, dive back into the game. Hannah hadn't believed her then, and longed to believe her now, but mingled fears constrained her.

She wanted new memories. New chances. New beginnings. Wasn't that why she'd come to Jamison in the first place?

You came here to hide. Nothing more, nothing less.

Then she wanted to stop hiding.

A rustle of wind brushed the leaves against the windows. The sights and sounds of fall leveraged her anxiety, but only if she allowed it to happen.

Determined, she sat forward, met Jeff's gaze and nodded toward the food. "Will you say grace or shall I?"

He reached for her hand and it felt nice to have Jeff grip

her fingers as he asked the blessing, his tone thoughtful, the strength of his hand a blessing in itself.

He smiled, released her hand and gave a delighted sigh as he opened the containers. "Since we're main-coursing this stuff, I had them pack two slices of strudel, too. I don't know about you, but I never have room for dessert if I eat a full meal, and Susan Langley's apple strudel is amazing stuff. I wasn't sure if you'd like raisins, so I got the one without them."

"Thank you, Jeff." She looked in his eyes and for the first time in ages didn't question the sincerity and integrity in another person, or the veracity of their smile. She let herself bask in the moment and realized how good she felt to be there.

So far as the east is from the west has He removed our transgressions from us....

She wanted to believe that, the sweet psalm anointing her, but she'd found out the hard way that simple faith was anything but easy.

And yet…

Something in Jeff's look and his manner made her want to take the chance she'd been refusing to contemplate for years.

"You'll know when," Lisa had promised, offering her professional and personal opinion before Hannah moved east. "And when it happens, seize the day. Grasp the moment."

Hannah hadn't believed her; the thought that time eases pain was too simplistic to embrace then, despite the therapist's assurance.

But maybe now…

"Try this." Jeff speared a piece of shrimp, leaned forward and held the fork up, his encouraging look somewhat boyish and endearing.

She shouldn't take the morsel. Sharing food was too personal, but she leaned forward, the moment charged with awareness. She paused at the last moment, rethinking her choice.

It's shrimp. Nothing more.

Hannah knew better, despite her recent holding pattern, like a jet circling O'Hare in a snowstorm. But she took the bite anyway. The combination of cream and spices was melt-in-your-mouth good. "That's amazing."

Jeff grinned. "I thought you'd like it. Try another."

She raised her fork, putting off another tidbit from his. "Feeding myself was one of my basic skills in college."

"Where I expect you did very well," he countered, following her lead, adeptly moving the conversation. "I did my undergrad and masters at MIT." His interested expression invited her to reveal the same about herself.

"I was at Penn."

"Philadelphia."

She nodded. "My father and stepmother live there. That got me the occasional home-cooked meal."

"Which always tastes better when you're away from home. And you never fully appreciate the things of home until they're gone."

Hannah knew that firsthand. Her parents had split up amicably just shy of her ninth birthday. Both had remarried. Both marriages were still intact, but she'd never had a place to truly feel at home from that moment on. No matter which home she visited, a level of disconnect followed her as she figured out behavior that suited her stepfather and stepmother, a slippery slope for a kid. She'd hedged toward perfect, swallowing emotions, pasting on smiles, unwilling to make a scene, skills that turned against her later on.

As a science lover, she understood the intricacies of adaptation. What she didn't quite get was how to turn it off and move ahead. And if she couldn't do that, then all the adjustments in the world were of little importance because mere existence couldn't equate with life. Ever.

"The quieter you get, the more I delve." Jeff sent her a pointed look, his eyes amused but direct.

Hannah raised her fork in salute. "I only reveal things on a need-to-know basis, Jeff." She leaned forward before hiking one brow. "And right now, all you need to know is that I'm amazingly grateful for this food. Thank you."

"And the company?"

Ah, the company. She smiled, raised a glass of water and dipped her chin. "Even better."

His grin said more than words as he sampled a piece of stuffed mushroom. Was his look of delight meant for her or the delicious food?

She wasn't sure but a big part of her hoped it was for her. That sent her onto dangerous turf, but for the first time in a long time it felt good to laugh and tease with someone.

Real good.

Success.

Partially, Jeff admitted to himself as he headed back toward Wellsville later that evening. They'd exchanged fund-raising ideas, scoped out the time frame and brainstormed how to bring the library project to the forefront of people's minds. Spring and summer offered many opportunities, but winter in their mountainous foothills narrowed the selections. If they could target the Farmer's Fair at the end of October, the Christmas Salute to Veterans concert in December, then the Maple Festival in March as their big fall/winter projects, they should have a successful launch. Throw in the direct-mail campaign and fundraising on the Jamison green on Sundays…

Jeff hoped it marked a strong beginning. His mother's ringtone interrupted his thought process. "Hey, Mom. What's up?"

"You know that Matt's back."

Jeff's gut tightened. "Yes."

"I've invited him to supper tomorrow night."

"Perfect. I'm busy."

"Exactly why I scheduled it then," Dana Brennan explained. "I won't have you boys fighting at my table, or have you make him feel like he's to blame for your father's actions."

Perfect. Just perfect. The prodigal comes home after two decades of doing whatever and gets the welcome-to-the-table speech while Jeff got the shaft. "I can lay plenty of his own actions at his door, Mom. He made sure of that twenty years ago."

"He's changed, Jeff. He grew up. And he paid his price."

"Tell that to Katie Bascomb. Every time I see her I remember that night, that weekend. He's lucky she wasn't killed."

"Yes. But Matt wasn't given an easy road to travel."

"And I was?"

Dana sighed. "That's not what I'm saying, honey. I know how rough things were for you and your sister. And maybe I tried too hard or stayed too long with your father, thinking he would keep his promises."

"Which he didn't."

"No. But you do, Jeff. You always have and I'm proud of you for it. I just wish…"

"That I would embrace your rainbow-colored world, forgive Matt and sing kumbaya? Didn't you just admit to trying too hard with Dad? I might be the one that looks like Dad, but Matt's got his personality down pat and I don't want to see you or Grandma get hurt."

"Or maybe you're protecting yourself."

"From?"

"Memories. Fears. Anything that reminds you of your father."

Jeff sighed. It had been a long day already, up early to get a jump on work Trent Michaels would have done if his foster father wasn't sick, but with Trent gone…

"I'm tired, Mom. While you're entertaining Matt, I'll be kicking off a fundraising campaign I don't have time for. That seems to be the trend lately—'If no one else can do it, ask Jeff.'"

"You know I'll help. And stop feeling sorry for yourself. You love going 24/7, it's intrinsic to your nature. And Grandma and I both appreciate your time and your devotion to the library project."

Right then, Jeff didn't feel appreciated. He felt put out, put upon and a little put down. "Good night, Mom."

"Night, honey. I love you."

"Yeah." He paused before adding, "I love you, too." He disconnected the call, pulled into his driveway and sat back against the leather seat, considering the current circumstances. His brain refused to work without sleep. He'd catch a few hours, then jump into the specs for a new Homeland Security bid that included the mobile surveillance units his team designed. The forthcoming eight-figure contract would push Walker Electronics another notch up the ladder of military supply companies, and that meant more workers, more production, more jobs and a stronger local economy.

But it stunk big time that his good-for-nothing brother got invited to dinner, because with the library meeting tomorrow, Jeff would be lucky to have time to scarf down a deli sandwich on the run.

Sometimes life just wasn't fair.

Chapter Four

"Jeff? May I see you a minute?"

The sound of Grandma's voice drew Jeff's attention in the library parking lot the next evening. He smiled and crossed the lot, surprised but pleased. "You're here. I thought you were attending that dinner for the Veteran's Outreach tonight."

Helen tipped a thoughtful look his way. "I decided it was more important to see you."

Her words puzzled him. "Except…we saw each other off and on all day."

"But not about personal things."

True enough.

He and Grandma didn't discuss family things on the job. And the only family things of note that had happened recently were Meredith's job loss and Matt's return. Since Meredith was avidly looking for a place to open a salon of her own, Grandma's visit could have only been spurred by one thing: Matt Cavanaugh.

Wonderful.

Jeff angled his head, silent. Waiting.

Grandma took his arm and headed toward the library. "Everyone deserves a second chance, don't they?"

He nodded. Shrugged. "Sure. It's the seventh, eighth and ninth that concern me, Grandma. Did he ask you for money?"

She paused and offered him a sharp, shrewd look. "First, it wouldn't be your concern if he did. I'm perfectly capable of making my own decisions and you need to respect that. Second…" Her frown deepened and she gave him a quick, appraising glance that said she was deliberately holding back. "You'll need to settle this thing in your head if Matt's moving back to town."

"He's not, is he?" Jeff read her expression and swallowed what he wanted to say. "Tell me you're kidding."

"He's looking for work."

"We didn't offer him a job, did we?"

Helen puffed an impatient breath. "What work does Walker Electronics have for a home builder? No, he's quite self-sufficient, but I suspect he'll be around awhile."

"Plenty of cause for concern right there."

Helen's look sharpened. "Matt's not the one I'm worried about."

Her words stung, just like his mother's the night before.

They weren't bothered by Matt's sudden reappearance? Then it was a good thing Jeff had enough concern for both of them. He shrugged off her comment, hid the hurt and angled toward the tiny library, which was in need of refurbishing. "I'm fine. You know that."

"Yes." She paused again, hesitant but straightforward. "And no."

"Yes," he countered firmly. "And this isn't a topic of conversation we can pursue right now." He straightened as a volunteer's car angled into the small lot. Fat raindrops began to pelt them. "I've got a job to do."

Helen stepped back, nodded and opened her umbrella. "You do. And that's the reverend so I'll just walk over there and say hi before we get started." She gave Jeff's arm a light squeeze before she headed toward Reverend Hannity's car, as if her touch would soothe the prick of her words.

She was worried about *him*.

Not Matt.

The incredulity of that cut deep. Right now he needed to get inside, compare notes and goals with Hannah, dust off his bruised ego and get to work fulfilling Grandpa's dream, a well-set library system throughout Allegany County. And he needed to do it with the polished veneer of a leader, ready to forge ahead, when what he wanted to do was…

His hands clenched. His thoughts jumbled and frustration climbed his spine, settling in somewhere along the back of his neck.

He had no idea, so he buried the angst as best he could and headed through the door, a part of him wishing Grandma had gone to the veteran's dinner as planned.

"Are we ready?"

Hannah gave her heart a chance to come under control at the sound of Jeff's voice. His kindness the previous night was a delightful new memory that had managed to interrupt her sleep. But tonight he sounded gruff, and Hannah was savvy enough to know that any guy could appear nice for an hour or two. Maybe Jeff had exhausted his limit the previous night.

She turned, tamping her reaction. From the dozens of wet splotches on his clothes, the promised showers had come to fruition. "You're wet."

"Rain does that." He peeled off an expensive-looking trench, then swept the room a glance. "I'd forgotten how small this place is because I use the Wellsville branch."

"And that's exquisite," Hannah acknowledged. The Howe Library was a shining star in the economically roughed-up town.

"We've really got our work cut out for us."

Did he realize his slight derision reflected her work for the past three years? She offered the tiny library a quick perusal. "It may be small, but it does the job."

"If it did, we wouldn't be here, Hannah."

"Ouch."

He huffed a breath, ran a hand across the nape of his neck, then shrugged. "I'm sorry. I didn't mean that the way it sounded, I just…" He stopped, glanced toward the exit and held up his jacket, pretending to head for the door. "Can we have a do-over? Please?"

No, they could not. "Unnecessary." She flashed him a cool, crisp smile. "Folders are on the table."

The door opened. Several committee members streamed in, lamenting the rain in mixed voices.

Jeff turned to greet them, his manner inviting, more like the guy she'd shared food with last night.

Just because he wears a suit, doesn't mean he's cut from Brian's cloth.

But he'd walked in here pretty tense and frustrated, and Hannah didn't do uptight or overwrought. Or driven, for that matter. Not anymore.

Jeff's attention veered left as another voice joined the group. Hannah watched as Helen Walker greeted people much like her grandson, offering a warm smile and a firm handshake. And having met Helen back when she interviewed for the librarian position and the other day, Hannah wasn't blind to the older woman's work-first focus and drive. But Helen's didn't bother her.

Jeff's did.

Because you're constantly comparing him to Brian. Move on. Forge ahead. There is nothing wrong with focus. Got that?

Hannah grasped Helen's hand. "Mrs. Walker, hello."

"Helen, please." Helen's grip offered warm assurance, the perfect handshake. "And as cute as this is, Hannah—" Helen let her gaze wander the children's corner, the faded carousel of computer stations and the narrow rows between labeled bookcases "—it's time we did better. You understand that, right? And how essential your input is to the success of the final product we hope to achieve."

Her words inspired Hannah's grimace. "I'm sorry I balked initially. I shouldn't have done that. Please accept my apology."

Helen beamed. "Accepted and forgotten. We all get a little intimidated now and again, don't we?"

"I suppose so."

Jeff shifted their way and indicated the school-style wall clock. "We should get started."

"Of course." Hannah offered him a polite nod and headed for her seat at the end of the table. He sent her an unreadable look as he took his place opposite her, the long library table creating a distance.

And distance is good, Hannah told herself, settling in. *Real good.*

"I love this concept." A primary school teacher raised Hannah's overview folder up. "Using the solar system to represent how the branches circle the main library in Wellsville is stellar."

A communal groan sounded at her joke. She grinned and turned Hannah's way. "Did you do this?"

"Combined effort," Hannah explained, feeling more like her old self than she'd expected. The realization buoyed her. "The analogy was mine. The graphics were all Jeff's."

"I love it," declared Helen from her seat midway down the table. "And what's more, Jonas would have loved it. The artwork embraces all the sciences, and that is the goal of a well-set library. So, Hannah…" Helen shifted her way. "Can you walk us through possible fundraising ideas?"

"Of course." Hannah waved toward the far end of the table. "If I can direct your attention beyond Jeff, I've got a PowerPoint presentation of ideas, and then we can see how the committee feels about them individually."

"Excellent." Helen's warm expression went from one end of the table to the other, her enthusiasm obvious. "Financial constraints meant we had to wait much longer than I wanted to get this drive started, and I've felt guilty about it. And guilt isn't one bit fun."

It wasn't. Hannah knew that personally. With all Helen Walker had to do, the idea that one out-of-the-way, dot-on-the-map library meant something… That showed a whole lot of character. And Hannah respected good character.

"Jenny, adding a booth to next summer's Balloon Rally would be wonderful," Jeff assured the town council representative toward the end of the meeting. "And I don't think it matters that we'll be beyond our projected fundraising date. Added funds secure future purchases, and libraries can always use help in that regard. Well, then…" Jeff scanned his notes, flipped a few pages and sat back, satisfied. "We did well."

"Very well," Hannah added, looking calmer now that the meeting had ended and nothing had self-destructed. Right until she looked at him, then the cool, flat facade fell into place. But then again he hadn't exactly been Mr. Friendly when he'd walked in tonight.

He stood, made small talk, then walked people to the door, feeling Hannah's eyes watching. Assessing. Probably figuring he was a total fake, pretending interest he didn't feel. On the plus side, the rain had stopped.

"Hannah, if you need anything at all, please call me." Helen gripped the younger woman's hands in hers. She leaned in just enough to show the sincerity behind her words. "Please."

"I will." Hannah's smile said Helen's authenticity bested her grandson's.

Helen headed for the door and nodded to Jeff. "I'll see you in the morning."

"I'll bring coffee," he promised, then turned back to Hannah, needing to close the evening on a positive note between them. Pinpoints of guilt prickled him for his earlier insensitivity.

He straightened his notes and his spine, slid his portfolio into his laptop bag and shouldered it before facing her. "I apologize if I was too blunt earlier. I had things on my mind, but I shouldn't have taken them out on you. Or this project. It was rude." He was ready to go home and collapse; the successive long days were wearing on him. "Thanks for offering to type up the notes and meeting minutes. If you email them to me once you've got them ready, I'll go over them with Grandma."

"Or I can 'cc' her a copy and spare you the time," Hannah suggested.

"She'll want to talk it out," Jeff told her. "She's very hands-on, as you can see."

"Then I'll forward them and you can proceed from there."

She kept her tone cool. Crisp. Concise.

Just what he wanted, right?

Except spending time with her last evening had put him in mind of other things. But those thoughts were best buried.

She'd readopted her business manner and kept her distance, sparing him from looking into those bright blue eyes. The dimmer lights by the library door kept him from seeing the sprinkle of freckles, or noting the long lashes, their shadow a curve against her tanned cheek. Obviously she hadn't read all the current warnings about skin and sunscreen, because her softly bronzed face and arms said she wasn't afraid to be in the sun.

He gave a quick wave as he went through the door, deciding not to linger with uncomfortable goodbyes.

She'd email him, he'd email her, they'd push forward.

Perfect.

But it felt much less than that.

Dismissed.

Hannah watched him go and was tempted to throw something. Standing in a room full of books, her choices were numerous. But she couldn't throw books. She loved books. Loved learning. Knowledge. Sharing that love with others, children and young adults.

At least she *had* loved it until circumstances blindsided her, stealing her livelihood, her heart and a share of her soul. Melancholy threatened, but she pushed it aside, determined to stay in the here and now.

She didn't like being shrugged off by the electronics wizard as if she were some ordinary business partner.

Which she was.

Or some underling who depended on him for her livelihood.

Which she did. Kind of. Since his grandmother was head of the library council and approved her hiring three years back.

But the fact that he made her feel like that was aggravating. Exasperating. She shut off the lights of the tiny house, set the lock and headed for her car. Usually she walked from her apartment to the Jamison Farmers Free Library, but she'd known she'd be late tonight, probably tired, and rain was in the forecast, so she'd driven over. She'd get home, sit down, hammer out these notes, email them to Jeff and be done with things until the various committee members got back to her with their plans. Then she'd compile them into a semblance of order, send them on to Jeff and move to step two for next week's meeting.

Easy.

She fumbled in her pocket for her set of keys and stopped, chagrined.

Not there.

She tried again, then groped for a nonexistent purse.

Nope, she'd left that home on purpose, wanting to be unencumbered.

No keys.

Either she left them inside…

Or she'd locked them in the car.

She went over to the car, pressed her nose to the glass and tried to scan the interior.

No luck. Darkness had fallen hours ago, the fall equinox behind them. The one lone dusk-to-dawn light was set near the library entrance, leaving this corner of the gravel lot in complete darkness.

Split. Splat. Split. Splat.

Fat raindrops began to pelt her head, her face, her arms. And of course she hadn't brought anything along since she was driving back and forth. No sweater. No hoodie. No sweatshirt.

Grumbling, she tucked the important papers under her shirt to protect them, and started jogging for home, the thin manila edges cutting into soft skin with every running step.

She had a spare key at home, but that thought didn't make her any drier, warmer or smarter at the moment. By the time she got home, fumbled her hidden key into the apartment lock and closed the door behind her, she was cold, soaked and fairly miserable, a combination that brought back too many memories.

Shoving aside mental images that had owned her for too long, she headed to the shower and let warm water ease the chill and the frustrations.

The images she left entirely up to God.

Chapter Five

Jeff spotted Hannah as he cruised down McCallister Street the next afternoon; the pretty blond hair was a giveaway.

He pulled over, opened his window and called her name.

She turned, surprise lighting her face. The way his gut clenched on seeing her told him that instead of waning, the appeal was growing. Of course, the fact that he was showing up out of the blue on his lunch hour to thank her for the copious notes she'd sent him might have something to do with that.

Polite, he told himself.

Nice try, his conscience replied.

He jumped out of the car, rounded the hood and opened the passenger door for her. "Come on, I'll give you a ride. It's cooking out here today."

She looked trapped but grateful. The midday sun was blazing hot, a late September anomaly. "Thanks."

"You always walk?" he asked as he climbed in the driver's side a moment later.

"Umm. No."

He frowned, then nodded. "That's right, I saw your car last night."

"How did you know it was my car?" She tilted her head, her freckles darker in the bright light of the noon sun.

"Because it was the only vehicle there when I left last night?" He shot her a grin, angled down Whitmore and pulled into the library lot along the curve heading toward Route 19. "Sitting right where it's sitting now. Car trouble?" he asked, brows bent, his look encompassing the car parked exactly where it had been fourteen hours before.

She sighed and made a face. "I locked my keys in it."

"Last night?"

"Yes."

"So you walked home? At ten o'clock?" He didn't try to temper the concern edging his voice.

She turned more fully, surprised by his reaction. "My options were limited. Because it was ten o'clock."

"You could have called me." The suggestion made her sit back farther, a touch of awareness brightening her features. But right now he was too busy thinking about what could happen to a woman alone on country roads at that hour. "I was minutes from here. I could have swung back, picked you up and got you home safely."

"Which was the outcome as you can see from my unscathed body." She waved a hand toward herself. "And since you were decidedly cool last night, why on earth would I have called you for help?"

"Because..." He paused. "Because I want you safe," he went on, meeting her gaze, letting his eyes say more than his words. "It was pouring rain before I got three blocks away. You had to be soaked."

"Drenched." She sighed, her face a mix of resignation with a touch of sorrow.

Why sorrow?

He had no idea, but a part of him longed to wipe it away, replace the look of anxiety with joy and youthful abandon. Although at thirty-five, youthful abandon had escaped him about twelve years ago, when his father's ignominious death marked the end of a dark era.

But something about being around Hannah made him want to embrace that lost joy. That family camaraderie. Since that was impossible, he'd try to figure out what was going on here. Looking at her, it seemed fairly obvious, but was that emotion or hormones?

Both.

"So you walked home in the pouring rain, then sat down and typed up copious notes for my benefit?"

"I like to stay on top of things." She shrugged as if it was no big deal.

Jeff had been in business long enough to know a good work ethic was key to success. Hannah's drive and determination belied her fragmented lifestyle. She obviously embraced her privacy, a concept he respected. He climbed out of the car and circled the hood, meeting her as she emerged. "Thank you, Hannah."

She glanced up, those blue eyes meeting his, a flash of awareness in her manner. She looked flustered again, only it wasn't the insecure agitation he'd seen before. This implicit nervousness stemmed from him, their proximity, the look he offered that probably said too much.

He leaned down, holding her attention, deciding direct and to-the-point worked best most of the time. "Spare me the lecture of how this could never work, we have nothing in common, we barely get along and you're not at a point in your life to consider a relationship with a stuffed shirt like me."

A tiny smile softened the awareness. "Thanks for saving me the trouble of the summation."

"Except…" He moved closer, crowding her space, watching her pretend he wasn't encroaching on her emotions, her equanimity. "I want you to promise me something."

"What?"

Those eyes, that summer-sky blue, with tiny points of ivory offering inner light. "If you ever have car trouble, locked keys, a breakdown, a flat tire… Call me. Okay?"

She raised her cell phone and waggled it, then headed for the library door. "A little tricky since I don't carry your number around."

He snagged the phone, ignored her protest and proceeded to program his number into the speed dial.

He grinned and handed her phone back once she'd unlocked the library door. "I actually stopped by today with a purpose in mind."

"Because men like you always have a purpose."

"Since when did that become a bad thing?"

"Not bad, predictable. What was this purpose that dragged you out of your office and brought you here in person when you have a perfectly good phone at your disposal?"

He maintained a strong, sincere expression. "To thank you for the notes. They're perfect and I realized from the time stamp that you stayed up late to finish them. And now I know that it was after you got soaked to the skin."

"No problem."

"I'm grateful, Hannah." He reached out as the door swung open and laid a gentle hand on her left shoulder. The feel of her sun-kissed skin was warm and smooth, a summer touch in the grip of fall.

Her look said she wasn't immune to the buzz and that almost made him take that last step forward, but they both knew that wasn't a good idea. The look she gave him, yearning mixed with caution, made him go slow, which was for the best, right?

A car pulled in behind his. A woman tooted the horn in welcome, and a young boy waved from the front seat, his face a blend of excitement and eagerness.

Hannah smiled, the anxiety erased, wiped out by the smile of a child. A part of Jeff's heart melted on the spot. He released her arm, stepped back and nodded toward the car. "One of your young suitors?"

Her grin delighted him. "This is Jacob. We're working together on some really cool projects and he had a half day of school today so we're meeting earlier than usual."

One of her tutoring duties, Jeff realized. The boy dashed up the steps, ignored Jeff completely and launched a hug at Hannah. "I got them all right except the one about the gasoline."

She laughed and squatted to his level. "I saw that. Two hundreds and a ninety average out to ninety-six." She watched as he absorbed what she was saying. When he nodded agreement, she ruffled his hair. "That's an A, kid. Pretty solid."

"An A." He turned and sent his mother a smile that she matched. "I got an A, Mom."

"I'm so proud of you, Jake." She stooped, planted a kiss to his hair, then shooed him inside before facing Hannah. "He has never been this excited about learning. Not ever. His teachers are ecstatic and his grades are wonderful. I can't begin to thank you enough, Hannah."

Hannah's smile said she expected no thanks. "That A says it all. Head on in, Callie. I'll be right there."

"All right." The mother smiled and nodded to Jeff, then stuck out her hand. "I'm Callie Burdick and that whirlwind was my son Jake."

Jeff shook her hand, nodded appreciation toward the boy and grinned. "Jeff Brennan. Hannah and I are cochairing the library fundraising for this branch. He's an excited whirlwind, for sure. I was just thinking that if my third grade teacher looked like Hannah, I might have paid more attention myself."

Callie laughed.

Hannah blushed, then scowled. "Don't you have a job to get to?"

"I do."

"Then might I suggest—"

"I'm gone." He switched his attention to the other woman. "A pleasure, Callie."

Callie nodded and swept them a look. "May I help? On the project, that is?"

"Of course." Hannah grinned, surprised but pleased. "We'd love it, Cal. Do you have time?"

"More than I'd like right now, and working on this would be a good distraction," the other woman admitted. "With Dad's construction business taken over by the bank, there's literally nothing to do right now except pray the economy improves and Dad can get back on his feet. Since I crewed for him and worked in his office, we're taking a double hit. Waitressing doesn't come close to covering the bottom line, so a well-intentioned distraction would be heaven-sent."

"We'd love your help." Jeff made a mental note to see if he could track down her father's business based on her name. The nice thing about small communities was the way they looked out for each other whenever possible. He turned back toward Hannah. "Can I call you later?"

"I'm swamped."

Callie flashed them an understanding smile before she headed inside.

Jeff understood *swamped*. "Aren't we all?"

"I'm here until four, then at the candy store until eight," Hannah explained. "And I have every reason to expect to be tired by then."

Remembering the time on her emailed notes, he nodded. "All right. Tomorrow?"

"No can do. I've got library hours in the morning, then I'm overseeing the mock-up of a weekend camper science project at Dunnymeade's Campgrounds."

"You work there, too?"

She glanced inside, her look saying she didn't want to keep

Jacob and his mother waiting. "They needed someone to help lay out their minicamp so I volunteered."

"You like science?"

Her expression told Jeff he was on shaky ground. "Yes."

He nodded as if he hadn't noticed. "Me, too. Hence the degree. Maybe we can experiment sometime? Together?" He grinned, lightening the moment, enjoying the bemused smile she shot him.

"My experimental days are over."

"We'll have to see about that." He smiled, winked and headed for his car while he scolded himself silently for more reasons than he could count. "I'll catch up with you soon."

"We have a meeting scheduled next week." Hannah tapped a nonexistent watch. "Soon enough."

Jeff laughed at her from across the gravel. "Should we make it a contest? See who caves first?"

"I never lose, Mr. Brennan."

"Neither do I, Miss Moore." He grinned, opened his door and met her gaze. "You're on. The first one to call or contact the other for reasons other than the library fund project buys dinner."

"You'd make me pay for dinner? On my salary?"

"To make a point, yes. We'll consider it valuable education."

"Since it won't happen we'll consider it moot. Goodbye."

She went into the library without a backward glance, at least not one he could see. But it wouldn't surprise him if she tipped a blind, watching him. Grinning.

And yeah, he knew there wasn't time to pursue this. Not now. *But if not now, then when? When will you let yourself embrace life?*

Reverend Hannity had done a series of sermons making that very point this fall. Thoughtful and thought provoking, his gentle words had tweaked Jeff's conscience. The work demands that used to nibble his free time now consumed it.

Was his dedication to work extreme?

The fact that he didn't want to answer that question said plenty. Sure, he'd grown up in the shadow of his father's misdeeds, and their physical resemblance was so strong that Jeff felt required to establish degrees of separation. He accomplished that by being honest, faithful and self-reliant, qualities his father could have embraced.

But chose not to.

Hannah was right. He should squelch this attraction and cite bad timing as the reason. He needed to cover for Trent while putting the company's best foot forward on current bids.

Plus, the girl wasn't interested. Correct that, she *was* interested, but didn't want to be and Jeff sensed that reluctance. He didn't need distractions or aggravations. Neither did she. And since they'd thrown down a challenge to see who'd cave first, maybe it was for the best if neither caved.

It wouldn't be easy to let things slide. And the thought of her walking home, even though it was only several blocks away…the image of her alone, on the streets, in the rain, the dark of night…

That brought out his protective instincts. But she'd made it this far without his help, his protection. The fact that he wanted, no, *longed* to help and protect needled him.

But he'd let it go. They both would. He knew she wouldn't call. If self-preservation was a lock, Hannah Moore turned the key long ago.

Sometimes God offered a distinct picture of right and wrong, and sometimes He let you figure it out for yourself. This time, Jeff was pretty sure of the message he'd been getting from Hannah.

Put it on hold, as much as it scorched his take-charge mind-set.

And with work tugging him in different directions, it might not scorch as much as he'd have thought.

Chapter Six

Hannah moved to the candy store counter and smiled at the teenage boy who walked in with his mother on Monday afternoon. He didn't return the smile, just gave a semi-embarrassed "what am I doing here" half shrug.

Hannah understood the adolescent gesture. When the woman moved off to examine preboxed candy, a note of desperation darkened the boy's eyes, a quick flash, as if weighing escape routes and finding them lacking.

A cold shudder coursed through Hannah; an icy prickling climbed her back, clawing her gut.

She stood on her side of the counter, wanting to move, wanting to help, frozen in the press of memories, the boy's stark look familiar.

The boy read her expression and jerked his features into a quick semblance of normalcy. Then he ducked his chin.

He's a kid, Hannah reminded herself as she stepped forward. *They're all a little whacked-out at this age. Puberty does weird things to kids' heads. You know that, Hannah. Get a grip.*

"May I help you?"

He shrugged again, glanced around, then settled a look on his mother. "I'm just waiting for her."

His detached tone told Hannah he wasn't here by choice. She nodded and raised a tray of freshly done candies. "Well, I've got a sampling here of some new twists on old favorites. If you'd like to try a couple for me, I'd value your opinion, sir."

Mixed emotions crossed his face, a hint of hope and pleasure marked with surprise. "Like, free?"

Hannah's laugh drew the woman's attention. "Absolutely free. The only way we find out what works for people is a good old-fashioned taste test, so you're my current guinea pig."

He smiled as he reached forward. Her banter had eased the hopeless expression she thought she'd seen. "I'll try this and this."

"Perfect." She nodded his way, then offered the tray to the woman. "How about you? Can you be tempted as easily as your son?"

"Stepson," the woman corrected too quickly.

Hannah felt the swift bite that took the wind out of the young man's sails. She wanted to give the woman a piece of her mind, but that would only make matters worse. The boy kept his gaze trained on the candy, but Hannah could read the set of his shoulders that said he couldn't wait to be old enough to be out of his current situation.

Holding the plate out, Hannah wrestled the Holy Spirit's attention with an SOS. *Cover him, Lord, soften him, shelter him, guide him, give him Your grace, Your courage, Your temperance, Your strength. Take this boy by the hand and the heart and carry him through whatever darkens his path.*

The boy shrugged and sent a sheepish look Hannah's way as he headed for the door. "I'll tell you which ones I like next time I come in."

Hannah nodded with appreciation. "Thank you…?" She ended the sentence on an up note, wanting his name.

He stepped outside and the door swung quietly shut behind him.

The woman sighed, tired, bored, rude. Hannah longed to smack her, but reminded herself she needed to cut the woman some slack, although right now that was the last thing she wanted to do.

"My husband tolerates far too much. If it were up to me he'd be doing more manual labor to teach him a lesson or two."

Hannah fought off a sharp retort, knowing it wasn't her place. Her heart went out to the boy. "Oh, he seems all right. Fairly normal for a young teen. What's his name?"

"Dominic."

"Nice. Strong."

"It's his father's name, handed down like some sort of crown. Ridiculous, really. Can you pack me a pound of mixed caramels, too?" she asked, pointing down the display case. "I'm hosting a dinner tomorrow night and chewy caramels might quiet some of the more annoying wives."

Hannah bit back words and nodded, filling the box quietly, not daring to speak.

The woman made a show of surprise at the final tally, handed over a debit card with obvious reluctance, then left the store in her designer shoes, her attitude a cartoon depiction of the fairy-tale stepmother.

Except this was real life and Dominic was on the receiving end of that harsh attitude.

Help him, God. Guide him. Soften the days, gentle his nights. Don't leave him alone, please.

Another customer walked in, followed by another. The late September day highlighted autumn's dance of color, summer's verdant green becoming fall's rainbowed majesty.

Hannah used to welcome fall, embracing the seasonal changes, the excitement of a new school year, ripe with opportunity. New classes, different students, fresh opportunities. Now she confronted the capricious season, willing herself through the beauty by way of prayer and self-therapy methods her psychologist taught her.

Day by day.

Seeing this boy's sorrow and angst, hearing the disdain in the stepmother's voice and seeing the kaleidoscope of color in the trees beyond the east-facing stores on Main Street drummed up a lot of memories.

But she disengaged herself from each twinge, taking care of customers and praying for strength, wishing for equilibrium, wanting more than anything else to move the clock back five years, to make a difference where it mattered most.

But that would never happen so she'd pretend to be brave and bold outside while her cowardly soul huddled within, wishing she'd done more, knowing she hadn't.

And she couldn't forgive herself for that.

Hannah felt the air change the minute Jeff walked through the door Thursday night. She had to squelch twinges of anticipation. Luckily, two other committee members walked in with him.

Perfect. Their presence precluded personal talk. She stepped forward and perked a smile that encompassed all three. "Good evening. I've got things set up at the round table tonight."

Jeff took her cue and stayed matter-of-fact. "And Grandma sent cookies from the Colonial Cookie store. Cookies you may have helped make."

Hannah kept her smile easy and her voice neutral. "I do the candy store more often now, so probably not. Although I've been known to warm up the cookie ovens at the bakeshop when Megan's shorthanded."

"Altruistic."

"More like thrifty," she told him. "Paying the bills. Hey, Callie, glad you could make it." Hannah shifted her attention to Jacob's mother as she hurried in, her hassled expression saying there weren't quite enough hours in a day.

"Glad to help, although I'll miss this place when it's all dolled up and fancy," Callie told her, grinning. She gave the small, cramped library a fond look. "This was the Farmers Free Library before I was born."

"And before I was born," added an older woman who followed Callie through the door, a newcomer to the committee. "And since I remember your mama pushing you in a stroller, Callie Marek, my memory stretches longer. But not with the same level of accuracy as you young folks."

Jeff stuck out a hand to the older woman. "I beg to differ, Miss Dinsmore. Your wealth of knowledge puts us youngsters to shame. How are you?"

She waved off his hand with a shrug of impatience. "I'm not being unfriendly, Jeffrey, but I've had a cold hanging on for the better part of a month and while common sense would say I'm not contagious, it also warns me not to be careless with others, so I won't shake your hand tonight."

"Is this the same cold you had in August?" he asked, his left brow shifting up.

"Or another one piggybacking the first. In any case, catching colds when you're a teacher isn't a bit unusual."

"But not getting better is," warned Jeff.

His concerned manner intrigued Hannah. Was this a family friend? A relative?

"Hannah, this is Miss Dinsmore, Wellsville's beloved high school science teacher." Jeff offered the introduction easily, his affectionate tone respectful but friendly. "There are few people here who haven't benefitted from her wisdom and patience during adolescence."

Science teacher?

A cool chill crept up Hannah's spine. "Nice to meet you." The other woman met Hannah's gaze with a pointed look of consideration before she softened her expression. "And you. I've heard a lot about you, my dear."

Jeff's look sharpened, but one of the other committee members drew his attention, interrupting the moment.

She knows.

Hannah met Miss Dinsmore's eyes and nodded, not willing to pursue the feeling but fairly sure she had no secrets from the wizened woman facing her. "Do you teach all levels?"

"Yes and no." Miss Dinsmore withdrew a chair and settled into it, a glimmer of discomfort darkening her features before she took a deep breath, let it out slowly and smiled. "I have over the years. Right now I'm doing bio and chem."

Hannah slid into the seat alongside her, reluctantly drawn. "I love biology."

"I know." Miss Dinsmore looked at her and broke her no-touch, I've-got-a-cold rule. She laid her hand atop Hannah's, commiserative. "You're quite gifted."

A sigh enveloped Hannah from within, a silent inner wince that didn't seem quite so harsh in Miss Dinsmore's presence. "Thank you. It looks like we're ready to get started." She nodded toward the opposite side of the table where Jeff stood waiting, a folder in his hands, his quick glance taking in the scene with Miss Dinsmore but too far away to hear their conversation.

Just as well.

Miss Dinsmore nodded, and turned her attention toward Jeff. Callie slipped in next to Hannah, her bright smile pushing harsh memories aside. Hannah was pleased that the old thoughts shoved off with barely a whimper, a good step forward.

Progress.

She thanked God for baby steps of strength while Reverend Hannity offered a prayerful request for wisdom and cooperation; his warm words advised open minds and prayed for open wallets to help augment the cramped library surrounding them.

And when Jeff's eyes sought hers at the mention of open minds and forward progress, his expression sent her heart into a crazy spiral of what-ifs and could-bes. Hints of breaking out and busting loose tugged at her self-containment.

And it felt good.

"So." Jeff stood with his back to the exit, arms folded, legs braced, facing Hannah and the now-empty room, seizing the opportunity to talk to her alone. "The meeting went well."

"Quite." Hannah finished gathering her notes, slipped them into her shoulder bag and jangled her keys. "And we finished early, which is always a plus."

"Except we're not quite finished."

She stopped halfway across the room, as if the short space marked neutral territory. "You had something to add?"

"You didn't call."

His words sparked a bemused smile. "Neither did you."

"Why?" He didn't move forward but he didn't step back either, his stance was solid, determined to find answers.

Hannah shrugged. "We've got jobs to do. There's no reason to let this—" she waved a hand from him to herself and back "—interfere."

"What is *this?*" He mimicked her hand gesture, his expression questioning.

Her gaze tightened. Her shoulders straightened. His question bothered her, but why? He had no idea.

He took the first step forward, figuring she was probably too stubborn to make the first move. He wasn't sure if that was good or bad, but it *was* intriguing. He halved the space between them in two quick strides. "Well?"

"We've got jobs to do."

"You mentioned that." He took another half step forward.

"And I can't deny that work's been pretty demanding on my end, with no letup in sight. Why didn't you call?"

"Because I'm hideously old-fashioned and think the man should call?"

"Nice try. What's the real reason?"

She studied him, something in her expression saying mixed feelings had become the norm rather than the exception.

That realization made him want to change things up, make her happy. Keep her happy. Which was silly because he barely knew her, and yet... Seeing her talk with his grandmother. With Miss Dinsmore. The way Callie Burdick opened up to her. All of this pointed to how special she was, while she tucked herself out of the way, skirting the edge of life.

"I'm not a big fan of heartbreak, Jeff."

A clue. He nodded. "Me either. But that's a big jump from a nice dinner, a few evenings together—"

She raised a hand to stop him and went all serious and cute. "Which seems presumptuous, I'm sure... Or just plain silly."

He shook his head. "It's not either. It's simple caution. But how do we know where this—" he did her hand gesture again, teasing her "—might lead if we don't talk." He moved forward. "Date." Another step put him within a hairbreadth of her, those blue eyes inviting him to drown in the depths.

"I don't date."

"Perfect time to change that." He softened his voice to a whispered invitation, then grasped her left shoulder with his right hand. "We have nothing to lose, Hannah."

She stepped back, eyed him, ran a hand through her hair and shook her head. "I have a lot to lose, Jeff. I don't take risks. I don't buy raffle tickets, I don't play the lottery no matter how much of the money goes to education. I play it safe and sound now. It's the best I can do."

"Now." He held his ground. Another piece to the puzzle.

"Which means you used to take chances. What made you stop?"

She didn't cringe, wince or do any of the moves typical of a wounded animal, yet he instinctively felt the moves unseen. She settled a look of pained strength on him, an expression that said she'd examined her options and chose the only one available.

And it wasn't him.

"Life changes people, Jeff."

No disagreement there. Life had certainly done a number on him, but he'd survived. "Doesn't free will give us the power of choice?"

She contemplated his words, glanced away, grimaced, then nodded. "Within reason. But sometimes those choices are beyond our realm."

"Only if we let them be." He closed the space she'd created with her small step back. "God puts that road before us, broken or clear, and then we make the choice of how to maneuver the path. Hurdle the potholes. Climb the hills."

"Some hilltops are inaccessible."

He shook his head, decided he'd said enough and gave her shoulder one last gentle grasp. "With the right shoes and training, all hills are attainable. How about dinner Saturday night?"

"I just said—"

"I'm ignoring your lame protests in favor of my desire to get to know you better. And you owe me dinner."

She straightened, shrugging his hand away, a half smile brightening her features. "I don't. I didn't call."

"You walked out on our first dinner together, meaning you still owe me a date."

"It wasn't a date so your reasoning is illogical."

"Really?" He grasped his laptop bag and winked. "My game, my rules. I say it was and we need a do-over."

"And if I disagree?"

"I'll pester you until you cave. You could—" he leaned her way as they headed for the door, smiling inwardly as she tried to hide the look of enjoyment his teasing inspired "—save us a whole lot of trouble and go out with me on Saturday. It's the weekend, we both have to eat, it's a perfect excuse to wind down before Sunday." He waited as she locked the door, tested the handle, nodded satisfaction and turned smack into his chest. "And we could talk." He dropped his gaze to her cheeks, her mouth, then raised his free hand to graze her chin ever so lightly. "Get to know each other."

"But—"

"Please?"

The little-boy *please* did it. She caved, her eyes searching his, saying more than she wanted them to, he was quite sure of that. "Okay."

He smiled, the whispered response exactly what he'd been hoping for. The fact that he had no idea why he needed to chase those shadows from her eyes wasn't lost on him.

Why was he drawn to a woman with issues?

Because she needed him. But didn't want to need him. And that raised the stakes.

Watching Hannah ease her aging car down the road, the memory of their banter fresh in his mind, he realized that a big part of her wasn't playing games, and that sobering thought meant he better make sure he was on solid ground himself. That was easier said than done.

He called in an order for sandwiches from the Beef Haus. By the time he pulled up to the curb, his growling stomach reminded him lunch had been a long time ago. A waitress smiled his way, grabbed a to-go sack and handed it to him. "Two beef on wecks with extra horseradish on the side and an order of fries, right?"

"Exactly," Jeff told her. He pulled money from his wallet and handed it over. "Here you go, and keep the change. I was hoping I'd catch you guys before you closed up."

"And you did." She smiled at him, then shifted her attention to someone behind him. "You're all set, Matt?"

"Yes. Thank you. I left money on the table, Gail."

She swept Jeff a quick look, then nodded, understanding. "I'll take care of it. Thanks for coming in."

"No problem. Great food. Brought back a lot of memories. Good night." He turned to acknowledge his half brother, his gaze steady. "Jeff."

"Matt."

Matt noted Jeff's bag with a glance. "Seems eating late is a family habit."

Jeff didn't want to share any habits with Matt Cavanaugh, but seeing Matt here, unexpectedly, resurrected his mother's words from last week. Moving on sounded great in theory. In reality, with Matt standing toe-to-toe with him?

Much harder.

Matt headed out the door. Jeff followed more slowly, giving Matt time to get to his truck and pull away, not wanting a confrontation this late at night. Maybe not wanting one at all. He climbed into his car, set the bag down and eyed the town.

This was home. His home. His place.

And his, an inner voice scolded.

Was his, Jeff corrected. And that was a long time ago. He gave up the right to call this home by breaking laws. Going to jail. Being a jerk.

A lot of kids are jerks, his conscience persisted. *Luckily, most of them grow out of it.*

Had Matt?

Jeff sighed. Christ had come to forgive man's sin by offering Himself in sacrifice. Embracing the cross. Out of grievous wrong had come great good, so why couldn't he look at Matt Cavanaugh without cringing?

Help me, Father. You've given me strength and focus, You delivered me from rough situations with my father, You anointed me with intelligence to create amazing things. Why can't I do this little thing, to forgive my brother?

Cool silence answered his prayer. The chill of October pushed thermometers down. He stared into the quiet night, sighed again and put his car into gear, not nearly as hungry as he'd been ten minutes ago.

[illegible faded text from previous page bleeding through]

Chapter Seven

"Jeff, is that you?" Delight brightened Dana Brennan's features as Jeff walked into his mother's house midday Saturday. "I was just telling Meredith I needed to see you and here you are."

He eyed the clock and sent her a not-so-pretend look of disbelief. "Since I said I was coming by, it's really not a big surprise, right?"

"You said you *needed* to stop by, not that you *would*, and I've been your mother long enough to know that work sometimes interferes."

He couldn't argue with that. He grabbed a handful of homemade pizzelles and followed her into the kitchen. "Where's the brat?"

"Seriously, Jeff? I'm thirty-two. I stopped being a brat last year." Meredith grinned at him from her spot at the island counter, a bowl of fresh green beans making her look way more domestic than she'd ever thought of being, but that was before she'd been dumped as the manager of an exclusive spa when the owner's daughter took over. Sometimes nepotism wasn't a good thing. In Meredith's case, it brought her home with little money in the bank, no furniture because she sold it rather than move it, and great hair. Jeff matched her grin, then scrutinized the bowl. "You're helping Mom cook?"

"She's trimming the beans so we can grill them," Dana explained. She settled a fond look on Meredith, obviously pleased to have her home. "I'm going to brush them with garlic oil and a dusting of salt and fresh-ground pepper. Wonderful stuff."

"It sounds good," he admitted, snatching a pair of beans to go along with the pizzelles. "I've never met a green bean I didn't like. So why are you playing kitchen domestic when you said you'd be hunting up possible sites for a beauty shop?"

"A salon, Jeffie, not a beauty shop. How fifties can you get?" She sent him a look of dismay, then shrugged. "I was examining possibilities with Mary Kay this morning, but we didn't find anything that fit my vision."

"How about your pocketbook?"

She made a face. "Since it's empty, Grandma's start-up loan and a mortgage will be my launchpad. I knew times were fundamentally tight, but I didn't realize that funds for small-business loans had dried like the Sahara."

"Grandma's okay with up-front money?"

Meredith trimmed the ends off the next pair of beans and eyed him, puzzled. "You work with her. She didn't tell you?"

Jeff shook his head. "We don't discuss personal stuff. If it doesn't involve Walker Electronics, I don't ask and she doesn't offer. We don't mix personal and business."

"Seriously?" Meredith smiled at him and Jeff realized it was the first smile that had reached her eyes since she'd come home weeks before. "That's classy of you."

He waved that off. "Just good sense, Mere. Why muddy water we've worked so hard to clear?"

Her smile faded and Jeff backtracked. "Wait, I didn't mean it that way, like your business would muck things up. It just seems smarter to keep things separate."

His mother leaned in. "Stop talking. You're only making it worse."

"I see that. Silence is my new middle name."

"Ha."

"So what brings you by?" Dana gave him a look as she chopped peppers with finesse. "Nothing serious, I hope?"

"You know I'm doing the library fundraising for the Jamison branch?"

Dana nodded. "Of course. I'm planning on being a two-time Austen sponsor."

"Say what?" Jeff exchanged puzzled looks with Meredith.

"You've established levels for donations, right?" Dana looked up, her expression saying her intent should be obvious.

"Yes. Lee, Twain, Alcott, Cooper, Austen, Fitzgerald."

Dana nodded as if her reasoning made perfect sense. "I wouldn't read Fitzgerald if you paid me, but I love Austen, so I'm signing on to be an Austen contributor twice. Once in my name, and once in honor of you and your sister. That way it's the same money and none of the negativity. Have you ever read an Austen book?"

Jeff didn't fake his shudder. "Not on your life."

"Read one and you'll understand." She waved a knife at him that looked more like a meat cleaver than a veggie dicer.

"Why so much for Jamison?" Jeff settled into the chair opposite her while he munched a bean. "You didn't give that much to the Wellsville branch."

"Two reasons." Eyes down, she chopped until a small mountain of green pepper stood ready to layer over a bowl of slightly warm Yukon gold potatoes. "Wellsville had plenty of donors because it draws from a bigger population and I knew they'd do fine once the idea took hold."

She was right. The Wellsville library was now refurbished, its terraced patio seating a work of art.

"Secondly, most of my friends are from Jamison. And your

dad and I were married there. I've got a lot of old memories in that little town."

Jeff knew they'd been married there. He'd assumed it was because his mother had been in the family way and they wanted to keep it quiet so they'd opted away from the beautiful cathedral-like church in Wellsville. He'd always wondered what would have happened if she hadn't gotten pregnant. It wasn't like he felt responsible for the whole mess, but if he hadn't been conceived, what would her life have been like? Would she have married his dad anyway, following a road of broken dreams and empty promises?

Knowing his mother's gentle heart, he recognized the likelihood; her hopeful nature was optimistic to a fault. And while Jeff had no memories of his father's early engineering brilliance, some of Neal's initial concepts had been the starting ground for later projects, so there was no faulting his mind. His weakness for drugs, gambling and women? A whole different scenario.

"We're planning a Harvest Dinner to wrap up October at the Farmer's Fair and I was hoping you would chair the food end of it. Nobody puts together a fundraising dinner to rival you, Mom."

Dana smiled with delight. "I'd be glad to. And if it's successful, maybe your committee could stagger a few more throughout the year. Something like that in January or February makes a great transition into spring."

Just the idea and enthusiasm Jeff was hoping for. He grinned and looped an arm around her. "I'll talk to the committee. Thanks, Mom."

"You're welcome." She liberally ground fresh pepper until dark specks dotted the vegetables below, the enticing smell jump-starting Jeff's appetite.

"I plan on helping with the later part of your campaign." Meredith interrupted his thoughts as she stood, rolled her shoulders, frowned at the high, barlike stool and settled her green beans into the sink for a quick rinse. "You've got stuff going on over the winter, right? And at the Maple Festival?"

"Yes."

"Well, count me in on that. I know I can't handle a lot right now with trying to find, develop and establish my—" she wagged two fingers of both hands in quotation marks "—beauty shop."

Jeff grinned. So did Dana.

"But once I've got things under way I can give you time. Donate services. Whatever you need as long as it isn't cold, hard cash. I'm leaving that one to you, Grandma and Mom."

Dana nodded. "We'll cover cash donations from the family. You donate great hair and nails. And massages. People love them these days."

Jeff wouldn't argue that point. A great massage after a strenuous workout?

Stellar.

He took his sister's cue, stood and bent to kiss his mother's cheek. "You smell like potato salad."

She grinned. "Story of my life. Let me know dates and times, menus, et cetera. I can come up with my own or follow the committee's direction. Either way works for me."

"Will do."

Jeff turned toward his sister. "Mere, love you. Let me know when you narrow sites down. I'll come and look them over for you if you want."

"I'd love it," she admitted. She blew him a kiss from wet hands. "And I'm getting together with a bunch of the gals tonight, so I'll most likely have any and all current info on you by morning."

He grinned and sent her a mock salute. "Lotsa luck. Nothing to tell."

She matched his smile with her own. "That's what they all say, honey."

* * *

Hannah eyed the clock, set down her brush of pink-toned white chocolate and took off her apron. "Meg, I've got to get this stuff to the post office before two. Are you okay here?"

"Fine. And make sure you leave time to get ready for your date tonight. And let me just add, it's high time you started dating. I don't think you've had a date in the three years you've been in town."

Meg was right, and hearing it said out loud made her sound pretty lame. Still… "You don't think it's risky for me to date Jeff?"

"I think it borders on ridiculous for two thirtysomethings to *not* explore the possibilities. Seriously, Hannah, do I have to spell this out for you? Ticktock, ticktock?"

Hannah couldn't resist. "So, speaking of biological clocks…"

Megan's grin said it all.

"Dork, why haven't you said anything??" Hannah rounded the counter and hugged Meg. "Why the big secret?"

Megan shrugged, but still looked delighted. "We agreed to wait until we got to three months along because my mother miscarried twice. We just wanted to be as sure as we could be that things were okay."

Totally understandable. Hannah looked at the wall calendar. "And?"

"Three months tomorrow."

"Yee-haw!" Hannah spun her around, gave her another hug, then headed back to the kitchen, laughing. "I knew it, of course, but I'm glad you finally owned up."

"Oh, I figured you did." Megan nodded ruefully. "Something about morning sickness and pasty white skin says so much."

"Yup. So. End of March?"

"Thereabouts. And Danny's family is over-the-top excited. My parents are dancing in the streets and Grandma Mary…"

Megan grinned, her face a telltale sign of her great-grandma's approval. "She's hoping for a girl, named for her, of course."

"Mary." Hannah smiled. The sound of the soft, Biblical name was a whisper on the wind, hinting new life, new beginnings and established roots. Wonderful things. "I love it."

"Me, too. Danny was a little goofy about it, thinking the name was kind of forced on me, but I love tradition and family heirlooms. And what's a better gift for a newborn child than a timeless name?"

"I agree." Hannah headed for the door. "I'll be back in a few minutes. Anything you want? Need?"

Megan shook her head, her look of satisfaction born from within. "Nope. I'm good."

Pure delight pushed Hannah's steps. Just shy of the post office, a voice called her name. She turned and spotted a certain science teacher. "Miss Dinsmore, hello."

"You remembered."

"Of course." She smiled and put a hand out. "Nice to see you."

"And you." Miss Dinsmore half smiled, half frowned at Hannah's left cheek. "Been working with pink frosting today?"

"Oh, no. Seriously?" Hannah scrubbed her hand over her cheek and sighed. "Wouldn't you think I'd know enough to check my face in the mirror?"

"Well, it's fine now," Miss Dinsmore assured her, falling into step alongside. "And my car is parked around the corner, so I'll walk with you, if you don't mind?"

"Not at all."

"Lovely day. A nice hint of cool and crisp, tinged with warmth, the sun still high enough to toast the air."

"For a few weeks yet."

"Yes." Miss Dinsmore breathed deep, her gaze trained on the kaleidoscopic hills that backdropped Wellsville. "I love fall."

Hannah was just about to agree, the words on the edge of her tongue, but then she realized it was an old feeling, now abandoned.

She *had* loved fall. And she never minded winter. As an athlete she'd embraced cooler days for multiple reasons, but fall's show of color, the chilled starlit nights, the wanton winds of change, tempestuous storms pummeling trees and homes... She'd loved it all.

"Fall's hard for you, I expect."

Hannah's suspicions were confirmed. Miss Dinsmore knew who she was. "How did you know?"

"Two ways. I was on the hiring committee for the library and your background check offered your history at Ironwood."

Hannah knew it would, but no one had said a word. Not to her at least. "And the second way?"

"I kept a scrapbook with my class back then of what you and your class accomplished. Your classroom projects on the effect of mood-altering meds on the human psyche were wonderful."

But not wonderful enough, Hannah thought, a wellspring of emotion surging upward.

"And the fact that so many of your students came to an understanding of the cooperative inner workings of the human brain and of nature versus nurture were just wonderful. Were they all honors students?"

"No." Hannah took a breath and paused, seeing the sights and sounds of Wellsville while her brain wrapped itself around memories of Ironwood High. "Most of them were regular students, although a lot of them were overachievers in things that may or may not have been school oriented."

"I've had my share of those." Miss Dinsmore nodded, agreeable. "We always called them late bloomers, and it's not a bad analogy in retrospect. Sometimes we tend to overanalyze what history has taught us are simple aberrations of the norm."

"Which is exactly what our study showed." Hannah sent her a look. "But then we learned the hard way that nothing is really simple."

"And that no one teacher, one school, one community has all the answers," Miss Dinsmore replied, matter-of-fact. "I trained myself to recognize that when I get a student at age fourteen, I have four limited years of influence on his or her life. The family has had fourteen years to mess the kid up or strengthen him." She stepped closer, stopped Hannah's progress with a firm hand and looked deep into her eyes. "In other words, it's not our fault. Rainbows occur because of a finite grouping of events dependent on time of day, angle of light, prismatic function and saturation. If it takes all those accidents of time to make such a natural occurrence, how much more must it take to twist a child's thinking into total lack of conscience?"

"You're saying it wasn't my fault." Hannah tilted her head back, eyeing the sky, visualizing Miss Dinsmore's arced covenant in her head. "And I know that fundamentally. But I can't silence the cries. Or the sounds of the gun being fired repeatedly while I did nothing to stop them."

"You kept safe those you could," Miss Dinsmore offered, empathetic. "No one could have saved them all, not in a human context. That's why we've got God." She shifted her gaze, then brought it back, an air of quiet satisfaction marking her expression. "I've worked here a long time. I've made a difference. I know that. So I'm doubly glad you've come along now. I don't believe in fate, Hannah, but I put great stock in God's plan. His timing."

Hannah smiled, a bit of her gloom slipping away with this open discussion. Funny, she hadn't realized that *not* talking about Ironwood kept the memories closer at hand. Somehow sharing this information and testimony made her heart and soul feel lighter. "Megan was telling me the same thing at the candy store just minutes ago. I'm going to trust that you've both been put in my path to knock some much-needed common sense into me."

Miss Dinsmore grinned. "Oh, I think you're well equipped with common sense, but when our emotional well-being gets broken, it's hard to rebuild. It takes time. Prayer. Patience. And a good-looking guy is never a bad thing." A look of female appreciation brightened Miss Dinsmore's aging features.

"A—" Hannah turned, saw Jeff approaching them looking both surprised and pleased, then tried to contain the blush of pleasure she felt at his approach, his presence, his easy but purposeful gait. "Hey."

"Hey, yourself." Jeff stopped short of them and angled them a look of mock suspicion. "This isn't an impromptu committee meeting, is it? With no quorum? No reading of the minutes? Aren't there rules about such things?"

"Would it bother you if there were?" Miss Dinsmore's fond expression marked him as a favorite, but that was no surprise. Jeff had charm.

Or was he just another glib schmoozer, standing on the backs of whomever, wherever, to get where he wanted to be? Hannah's past record said her judgment in men might be off.

"Not in the least, especially with such lovely ladies."

Hannah made a choking sound and stepped back, only half faking. "Is that the best you've got?"

He settled a look on her that said plenty. "I'm saving the best I've got for our date tonight."

"And on that note—" Miss Dinsmore winked at Jeff, smiled at Hannah, patted her hand and gave it the lightest squeeze of understanding "—I'll leave the antics of youth to the young. Nice seeing you, Hannah."

"And you, Miss Dinsmore."

"Jane, please. For most of the area I'll always be Miss Dinsmore, but I'd love for you to call me Jane."

"Then I will, Jane." On impulse, Hannah reached out and hugged the older woman. "Thank you."

"No thanks needed."

Oh, but there were. They both knew it. Hannah appreciated Jane's gentle compassion for what it was. God-sent. Perfectly timed. They exchanged smiles of understanding.

Jeff turned her way, his expression quizzical, inquiring and totally good-looking. "You girls were discussing...?"

"Men."

"Ha."

Hannah grinned, turned and continued toward the post office just to see if he'd follow.

And he did.

"Any special men?"

"I don't know any special men."

He faked a shot to the heart. "'Teach not thy lips such scorn, for it was made for kissing, lady, not for such contempt.'"

Hannah laughed. "You like Shakespeare?"

"Some, not all. Great quotes, though."

"I'm a Franklin fan myself."

"Sage, science and certainty. Your Philadelphia roots are showing."

"A little." Hannah shrugged. "Since my father works for the university, my tuition was reduced, and he's got a pair of rental properties near campus so I didn't have housing expenses."

"That's a huge plus right there. Sweet education, Hannah."

"It was." She stopped just shy of the post office and turned his way, determined to keep this light. "So, about tonight—"

"Wear the blue. Please."

"Whereas I was thinking of canceling."

"Nope." Without a moment's hesitation he leaned in and

scraped a gentle kiss to her cheek, his lips grazing ever so slightly. The spontaneous gesture tweaked everything she'd put on hold a few years before, sedated emotions resuscitated by his gaze, his voice, his touch. "No chickening out. Promise?"

A part of her wanted to do just that, but another part longed to push aside old pain and shadowed loss. "I'm not a chicken."

"Then don't act like it." He said the words lightly, but the challenge shone through his eyes and the set of his jaw. "I'll pick you up at seven-thirty."

"Eight."

"Nope. I'm not losing a half hour with you if I don't have to. Grandma Mary's closes at six on Saturdays—that's plenty of time for you to get home and do whatever it is women do. And since God gifted you with good looks, I'd say your prep time is minimal. Seven-thirty. And dress casual. In the blue top." He stepped back, raised a hand in salute and strode away, leaving her watching. Waiting. Wondering.

But smiling.

And when he turned at the corner, he caught her watching his retreat. He grinned and winked, his confident attitude part bane, part blessing.

But sometimes confidence equaled selfishness, and she didn't dare let herself mistake one for the other again. Since she was obviously drawn to strong, successful types, men not unlike her father, she needed to be careful in matters of the heart. Her parents got along quite well despite their failed marriage, and their second marriages had both worked out so far.

But the little girl inside Hannah wanted the happily ever after, a knight in shining armor.

She finally felt like she belonged in Allegany County. She loved Wellsville; its gradual resurgence sparked all kinds of new business ventures. And Jamison was too sweet for words, the historic town embracing its past to provide for its future.

One broken heart could taint all that. When she was on her own, she could drum up a gazillion reasons why exploring this attraction to Jeff Brennan made no sense at all.

Ten seconds in his presence chased them all away.

So, okay. She'd go out with him tonight. Spar with him. Laugh with him. Have an easy conversation with a sharp, good-looking guy who made her heart jump at a simple word or a long, slow look.

But no way was she wearing the blue.

Chapter Eight

"You wore it." He hoped his look of appreciation said more than his lame words. "Thank you."

"It was the only thing clean."

"I don't believe you for a minute, but I refuse to gloat because good guys don't do that on a first date."

She shifted her position to meet his gaze. "I told you that other fiasco wasn't a date. So now you agree."

"Now that I've got you in my car for a real date, I concur. But it got you here, and that was not an easily won battle."

"Nothing's been won, Jeff. We're just…going out. Tonight. On one single date."

"Honey, every long-term commitment starts with one single date, doesn't it?"

"Or a guilty verdict by a jury of your peers," she shot back, her look saying she wasn't sure which was worse, dating him or serving a long-term sentence in a federal penitentiary.

He laughed out loud. "Either way, I've got you here. Now what am I going to do with you?"

"You said casual, so that limits your possibilities. And don't tell me you don't have every minute of tonight planned out. Guys like you always do."

"Guys like me…" he mused, keeping his eyes on the twisting road, but letting his voice weigh her word choice. "Who hurt you, Hannah?"

"Off topic."

"Call it a change of subject."

"Then consider it off-limits."

"For now."

"Jeff, I—"

She twisted in her seat. Once again he knew not to push. "How do you like your steak?"

"I'm a vegan."

"Wrong answer."

"I don't eat meat for humanitarian purposes."

He lifted a brow. "Since this morning when you wolfed down a bacon, egg and cheese muffin?"

"You're stalking me?"

He smiled, amused. "If stalking means I passed you on the street as I was heading to my mother's place, then, yes, I guess I am." He eased the car onto the entrance ramp for I-86 and headed west. He shifted the car, then his attention. "I didn't mean to put you on the spot, so food seemed a safe change of subject. Okay?"

"Maybe."

"Pretty please?"

"You're such a little boy inside. How did your mother resist your charms?"

"Didn't. Still doesn't. You'll find that out when you meet her. She's doing a double Austen sponsorship for the library and she's agreed to head up the food organizing for the Harvest Dinner."

"Wow."

Jeff frowned. "You didn't ask why a double Austen? I did."

Hannah noted the quizzical look and had to remind herself to take a breath. Even in profile the guy was a stunner. Great hair, strong forehead, laugh lines edging his eyes, perfect nose, square jaw. Jeff Brennan was every woman's dream choice to father their children. She cleared her throat and the imagery of two Jeff Brennan "Mini-Mes" wearing matching polos in her head. "She picked two Austens because Jane Austen was an amazing female novelist who set the bar for great romantic comedy and women's fiction. Do you know anyone who reads Fitzgerald?"

"Lots of people."

"Anyone you'd like to spend more than five minutes with?"

He grinned. "There you have me."

"Exactly." She pressed forward to make her point, humor coloring her tone. "Your mother sounds quite astute to me. And I like my steak medium rare. With onion rings."

"The only way to eat it." He reached out a hand to cover hers, just for a moment, but long enough for her to feel the blanket of warmth and zings of attraction rolling through her system.

Why him?

Why now?

When I was waiting quietly for the Lord, His heart was turned to me, and He gave ear to my cry. The sweet psalm enveloped Hannah, words of promise and patience.

Part of her felt undeserving, but these last few weeks had diminished the old negativity somewhat. Without the shadow of guilt looming like a gathering storm, she saw possibilities with greater clarity, the prospect of a future she'd denied herself to this point. "And do they have baked potatoes?"

Jeff smiled. "Idaho or sweet?"

"Either."

"They do. Are they on your training regimen?"

"I don't have one."

"Anyone who runs daily has one whether they recognize it or not."

"Not true." Hannah settled back into the seat and watched him. "I run to pray. To think. To absolve."

"Penance?" The tiny clench to his jaw said he had read too much into her statement. Or maybe just enough.

"I prefer the term *therapy*. I keep it controlled because I know I'm a little OCD. I like to do my best at everything and that can become obsessive. So I don't allow it to."

"Hence the onion rings and baked potato."

She grinned in agreement. "And don't forget dessert."

His smile said more than words could. "I'm looking forward to it, Hannah."

She waved a hand as they angled onto Route Sixteen. "I've never been to Olean."

"Seriously?" He glanced her way, the quieter road allowing him more leeway. "How long have you lived here?"

She hedged. "Three years."

"Where do you shop?"

"Wellsville. Jamison. Online." His expression said her response surprised him again, prompting an explanation. "I don't shop much."

"Another anomaly."

"Not true. I just have simple needs."

His appreciative look dispelled her twinge of concern. "In your case, simple says style." He pulled into a parking spot, climbed out, rounded the car and opened her door, the action old-fashioned and sweet. As she stepped out, he reached for her hand and held it overlong, his warm expression smiling into her eyes, her heart, thawing a corner she'd kept on ice for too long. He winked, grinned and tugged her toward the Millhouse. "Let's eat. I'm starved."

She couldn't help but smile back. He tugged her closer and swept a gentle kiss to her cheek. "You're amazing, Hannah."

Right then she *felt* amazing, invigorated by his attraction. For tonight she'd put aside concerns that echoed from her disaster with Brian. For tonight she'd dwell in the here and now, a move that seemed easier in Jeff's presence. For tonight, she'd be Hannah Moore, librarian and fundraiser, out on a date with a delightful man. For this one night, it would be enough. And it was, for about thirty seconds, right up until they stepped inside the gracious and updated eatery in the former grain mill storage facility.

"Mr. Brennan, good evening."

"How are you, Maggie?" Jeff smiled at the hostess.

"Fine, sir. I've set aside the customary table."

"Thank you. Maggie. This is my friend Hannah Moore."

"Miss Moore." Maggie extended her hand. "Is this your first visit here?"

"Mine? Yes." Hannah gave Jeff a pointed look that inspired his grin.

"Whereas my *family* has been coming here for years," he cut in. "Grandma grew up in Olean and she and Grandpa liked to bring us here for special occasions. Birthdays. Holidays. Family reunions."

"And your grandmother is well?" Maggie asked as she led them to a quiet table.

"Quite well. And your family?"

"All fine." She waited as Jeff held out Hannah's chair. When Jeff took the spot alongside Hannah, she sent him a relaxed grin. "And I know business is booming for Walker Electronics. I read the feature article in last Sunday's *Herald*, but I'm glad to see you get away from your desk now and again."

"This coming from a woman who works every holiday known to man," Jeff quipped back.

Maggie acknowledged that with a wry smile. "Too true. Family businesses are nothing to be taken lightly. But a nice heritage, all in all."

"It is."

Was it? Hannah wondered. The thought of Maggie working every holiday, the rush of business on weekends... There was no such thing as a weekend off in the restaurant business, but Maggie's words said something else.

She saw the work, the dedication and the diligence as part of her heritage, and that put a new slant on Jeff Brennan's ambitions. Inheriting a family business would come with no small level of responsibility, and that made working his way up the ladder of success more amenable.

A college-age waiter approached them for their drink orders. Jeff sat back, letting Hannah take the lead. "Do you serve lattes?"

The young man nodded. "Flavored?"

All the better. Hannah smiled. "Yes, please. Caramel?"

"Of course. And you, sir?"

Hannah leaned closer. "Someone who doesn't know you. Must not be part of the family."

Jeff smiled, grasped her hand and squeezed before answering the waiter. "Regular coffee, please. And I think we're going to forgo appetizers tonight because the young lady mentioned a hankering for dessert later."

"Or now." When Jeff turned her way, she quipped, "Life's short. Eat dessert first."

"Whatever you'd like, Hannah."

His easy words melted another corner of her taut heart. Something in his comfortable gaze, his winning manner, his gentle touch reminded her this wasn't Brian.

And then he withdrew a vibrating cell phone from his pocket, negating the little glimmer of reassurance she'd grabbed. He scanned the phone, let the call go to voice mail and turned the phone off.

Now she felt guilty. What if the plant needed him? What if some very important person had to wait to talk to Jeff and then called another supplier instead? She reached a hand toward the phone. "You can keep it on."

Jeff swept her and the phone a look before slipping it into his jacket pocket. "Why?"

"In case something important happens."

"Then they'll leave a message and I can check it later.

And the plant manager has Grandma's numbers, as well. And Trent's. We're covered."

"But Trent is out of town."

Jeff nodded slowly. "Yes."

"And what if your grandmother falls asleep or something?"

"Then she'll awake to the same message I find later. What's this all about, Hannah?"

She frowned, not sure herself. "I just don't want you to think you can't work if you need to."

"Well. Thanks. I think. What if I'd rather spend the evening talking with you?" He leaned back but kept her fingers loosely in his. "Getting to know you? Teasing you?"

"I'm not interrupting something important?"

He eased forward, lamplight softening the strong planes of his face. "Hannah, you *are* something important. For tonight, everybody else goes on hold. Not you."

By the time they got to dessert, Hannah realized she shouldn't have jumped to conclusions about Jeff Brennan, and that he might be just about the nicest guy she'd ever met, which might make holding to that just-one-date scenario a little tricky. Or downright impossible.

He'd wanted to get to know her better tonight.

He had, somewhat, but her reaction in the car on the way to Olean had cautioned him to hold off. Take his time. And since taking time with Hannah wasn't exactly a hardship, Jeff was okay with that for now.

He pulled into the driveway of her apartment house, switched off the engine and rounded the car to walk her to the door.

"I had a great time tonight." She withdrew her keys from her bag and smiled up at him. "Although that crème brûlée was probably an indulgence that will push me to an extra two miles of running tomorrow."

Jeff laughed. "This from the lady who doesn't have a training regimen."

"It's not a regimen. It's…common sense."

"Uh-huh." He stopped talking, letting his eyes wander her face, her eyes, her mouth. Settling there, wondering what it would be like to kiss Hannah, then deciding that wondering wasn't enough.

Her gaze flicked up to his, and he saw his question reflected in her pretty blue eyes. "Hannah."

Her answering expression offered silent permission. Jeff lowered his head, his hands gently grasping her shoulders, the nubby feel of her tweed wool coat a kiss of fall while Jeff lingered over a different kind of kiss.

Sweet. Soft. Warm.

The adjectives that filled his mind softened his heart; his worries about work, time and Matt disappeared in the wonder of kissing Hannah. And when he stopped, he didn't pull away, couldn't pull away. He embraced her in a hug, one hand cradling the back of her head, the other arm wrapped around her, glad they'd taken this step.

She dropped her forehead to his chest, then eased back. "Thank you for a lovely evening."

"It was fun. And the kiss speaks for itself, I hope."

Her blush said it did.

Jeff straightened his shoulders and tweaked her nose. "Can we plan the next date now, or do you have to put me through the wringer again?"

She thought a moment, then arched a brow. "Church in the morning?"

He ahemmed out loud, daring her to smile.

She did.

"Big step."

"I'm feeling braver by the minute."

"I see that."

When he took a few seconds too long, she stepped back,

lifting her left shoulder in a light shrug. "Sorry. It's one of my litmus tests and you just failed."

He gripped her shoulder, not allowing the retreat. "I wasn't hesitating on saying yes or no. But which one? Yours or mine?"

"Oh."

"Yeah. Oh."

"Mine," she declared, sure and certain. "You're the guy, you're supposed to go the distance. And Reverend Baxter is a sweetheart."

"And Reverend Hannity isn't?"

"Since they're related, the point is moot. And I'm second-guessing the invitation in any case."

"Rude, Hannah. No take-backs allowed."

"Who's making these rules?"

"We are." He leaned forward, wanting to kiss her again, knowing he'd best refrain.

"So you're in?"

"Their service starts at ten?" At her nod he winked and gave her hand a light squeeze. "I'll be here at nine-thirty. Be prepared."

She frowned, confused. "For?"

"The talk and speculation. A marriageable man and woman walking into church together in a small town, well…" He let the twinkle in his eyes say the rest.

Her composure wavered. Her expression stilled. "I didn't consider that."

He shrugged. "No big deal."

Maybe not to him, but it was huge to her. Hannah stepped back. "No, it *is* a big deal. If I'd been thinking clearly I'd never have suggested it."

He'd been edging toward the step, but now he moved forward again. "Are you afraid to be seen with me, Han?"

The nickname almost pierced her armor. No one besides

her Grandma Grady called her "Han." Until now. "It's not smart. Not at this stage of the game."

"I don't play games."

Um, right.

Maybe guys like Jeff and Brian finagled so often, they didn't see it as game playing, but Hannah refused to be maneuvered ever again. She took a firm step back. "I had fun tonight. A lot of fun," she admitted. She glanced left, then down, bit her lip and drew her gaze back to his. "But remember what I told you? I don't take chances. I don't guess the sure thing because it doesn't really exist. Maybe we can go out again sometime, but maybe we should just smile and nod, say we had fun, part ways and leave it at that."

His expression shadowed. A hint of reluctance darkened his eyes. But then he squeezed her shoulder lightly, nodded and stepped away. "You're probably right. Thank you for a wonderful evening, Hannah. I had a great time."

"Me, too."

She let herself into her small apartment. The neighborhood was silent in the cool fall night.

Her phone blinked a welcome as she crossed the room. She lifted it, pressed the code for her voice mail and smiled when she heard her younger brother's voice. "It's a girl! We named her Caitlyn Jean, for Mom, of course. She weighs seven pounds, two ounces, she's twenty inches long and Leah says to tell you she looks like you, which is perfect because we'd like you to be her godmother. Are you available in late November for a baptism?"

Hannah glanced at the time, decided congratulations would have to wait until morning, then slipped into the big easy chair she'd found at a moving sale up Route Nineteen.

Tears stung from nowhere, part joy for Nick and Leah's news, part pity party, wondering why she'd just turned away from the nicest thing that had happened to her in years. Was she totally crazy or just a little unsure of herself?

She didn't know anymore.

Going to church with Jeff wasn't earth-shattering. It would be nice. Typical.

Had she contained herself so long she'd forgotten that ordinary, customary things weren't out of the norm? Perhaps.

Time to change that. She swiped her hands over her cheeks and headed for the bedroom.

She'd told Jeff no in no uncertain terms, but a woman's prerogative was to change her mind. To that end…

She'd go to services at Good Shepherd tomorrow. Reverend Baxter would totally understand since Reverend Hannity was his father-in-law.

Now the big question would be what to wear since she'd already worn the blue…

With work demands pressuring him, Jeff almost didn't make the longer drive to Jamison when Wellsville churches were more convenient.

But he loved Reverend Hannity's homilies, so he'd cruised up Route Nineteen, figuring he'd make up time later.

He was glad he did when Hannah slipped into the worn chestnut pew next to him wearing a fall floral dress shot with bronzed thread that sparked light when she moved; her thin ivory sweater a tribute to the cool fall morning.

He edged closer, facing forward, part of him wondering if this was a good idea while another part warned him not to blow it. "You caved."

She nodded, thumbing through the prayer book, her face serene. "I did."

"And you admit it." He colored his whispered tone with surprise, pleased when her lips quirked up in a smile. "That's a big step forward."

She turned and looked up at him, right at him, her gaze making him feel ten feet tall and hideously unprepared, an odd pairing. But then, he'd already figured out that Hannah was no ordinary woman. Soft, lilting notes of a flute stopped her comeback, the gentle call to worship commanding in simplicity.

He'd have to work to concentrate this morning. He'd figured that out the minute she took the seat alongside him. His urge to shelter and protect elevated to "high" in her presence.

Why was that? He snuck a glance left and sighed quietly, noting the dip of her chin, the sweep of dark lashes, the soft, slow blink she did when lost in thought.

It didn't matter why. They were in the getting-to-know-you stage, except he knew next to nothing about Hannah while she'd learned a great deal about him.

But did she? his conscience scolded. *Did she discover anything of substance, or just the face you want the world to see? The strong, successful good guy who's nothing like his father.*

Except you are. And you know it.

Jeff shoved the admonition aside. He wasn't like his father, despite the mirror image. He'd worked strenuously to prove that, day by day.

And he'd keep doing it, making sure the world understood that Neal Brennan had passed on nothing more than a last name.

Well, there is that little wrinkle of an illegitimate half brother back in town.

Jeff fumbled with the songbook as the congregation stood, trying to put thoughts of his father aside, but Matt's presence in the area made that harder to do.

A light, chill rain started midservice, the steady sound drumming on the church's roof. "Did you walk?" Jeff asked when the service had concluded.

Hannah tugged her sweater closer. "Yes, but it's not really cold. I'm fine."

He sent her an "are ya serious?" look before pushing open the back door of the old church. Reverend Hannity stood on the broad top step, only partially covered by the overhang.

He greeted people with one hand clutching an umbrella. Jeff cast the umbrella a wry look. "Change is in the air, it seems."

"In many ways." The reverend swept the pair a smile.

Hannah's shoulders tightened.

Jeff defused her reaction with a light shoulder nudge. "I was referring to the weather."

The reverend's smile deepened. "Duly noted, of course. My vantage point on the altar allows me greater perspective so I find myself aware of subtle change before the majority of people. But sitting in church together? That's like putting your new friendship on the JumboTron at a football game."

"Speaking of which, there is a four o'clock game today and I've got work to do if I want to catch it." Jeff raised his hand, indicating his watch. "Have a good day, Reverend."

Reverend Hannity reached out and grasped Hannah's hand, his expression intent. "While I don't have the youthful verve and vigor of my son-in-law across the way—" he angled his head toward Holy Name where his daughter and son-in-law served "—I've got age on my side. Wisdom. And a wife who makes great cookies. Thanks for coming over, Miss Moore."

His sincerity softened the set of her shoulders. She smiled, a small dimple flashing in her right cheek. "My pleasure, Reverend. You won't tell, will you?"

He grinned. "Oh, I will. I'll brag it to the heavens to keep that son-in-law of mine humble. And if my team wins today? All the more reason to crow."

"The stadium will be washed in red, white and blue this afternoon. You're not going to the game?"

The reverend shook his head. "I go once a season as a gift from my wife. Stadium crowds get rowdy and I can jump up and shake my fist at the TV screen in the rectory with no fear of knocking over someone's soda. Other than my own."

"And the living room is climate controlled. Definitely a

plus as the weather turns." She smiled up at him and Jeff watched the pastor's smile bloom.

"Never a bad thing at my age. You folks have a nice day, okay?" The hint of blessing in his tone reflected the gentle look in his eye as he released Hannah's hand.

"We will." Hannah started toward the parking lot. "You, too."

"See you on Tuesday night, Reverend. We've got that council meeting at seven, right?"

"I'll be there."

"Good. Between you and me maybe we can keep Hank's subdivision off the auction block."

The reverend frowned. "I don't think that's possible, but I've been praying for a good outcome all around. Sometimes the worst wrongs produce wondrous good."

Christ's life epitomized the saying. Jeff nodded. "I can't argue that. See you then." He loped down the stairs and across the lot until he caught up with Hannah. "You know football?"

"I have a father, a stepfather and a brother. It was inevitable."

He grinned, grabbed her arm and headed toward his car. "Hop in. I'll drive you home."

"It's a five-minute walk and the rain's letting up."

"It's cold and you're only wearing a sweater. In." Before she could set her face in what he was coming to recognize as pure stubbornness, he bent a smidge lower and met her gaze. "Please?"

The *please* did it. She smiled, rolled her eyes and climbed in, but she was pleased he insisted. It showed in the curve of her jaw, the twinkle in her eye. "Breakfast? My treat."

Like he was about to let her buy him food on the slim pay-checks she brought in from two low-end jobs. Right. In any case...

He grimaced, reluctant. "I can't. We've got a final bid due

tomorrow and I've got to number crunch today, make sure I'm on target. And then there's a second one due on Tuesday. Trent's due back then, but not soon enough to shoulder any of this."

"Of course."

"Normally it wouldn't be a problem," he began, then wondered why he felt the need to explain. Could it be because she'd edged away the moment he cited his work schedule? That she'd taken a dislike to his responsibilities?

With military contracts, time equaled money and sometimes lives. Jeff took both seriously, knowing the future of Walker Electronics and Allegany County loomed brighter with the continued partnership with the armed forces. Trent's vision had become the new normal, and Jeff couldn't let anything interfere with that. Too many people depended on them for paychecks, benefits, opportunities for advancement. Not to mention the soldiers in the field, manning front lines, whose communications capabilities might mean life or death.

He pulled up in front of her apartment not sure what to say, an unusual circumstance for him. She climbed out before he could round the front of the car. He caught up with her as she climbed the first step and caught her hand. "You're mad."

"I'm not."

He held tight to her hand and just waited, silent, watching her. She sighed, blew out a breath and eyed the dripping trees. "I understand you have responsibilities. I'm sorry for trying to infringe on them, Jeff."

Part of him wanted to turn the clock back ten minutes and just say yes to breakfast.

Although no way would he let her buy.

But another part of him recognized the hurdle she'd erected.

Yeah, he worked hard. He had to, partially to continue Walker Electronics' growth and partially to repair the family name. And even harder right now because Trent was gone.

But he didn't feel compelled to justify any of it. That rubbed him the wrong way. His work ethic was part and parcel of him. It wasn't about to change.

She was obviously unsympathetic to that.

He stepped back, a sense of déjà vu blindsiding him, because hadn't they just done this same dance last night? And come to the same conclusion?

She beat him to the parting line. "Thanks for the ride home. I appreciate it."

"Anytime."

They both knew he didn't mean it. She'd put up a barrier he wouldn't try to scale. Hard work and industry were part of him, a piece of the whole.

Her reaction said she only dealt with fragments.

Jeff wanted the whole pie graph. He headed back to the car, waved his hand, climbed in and refused to beat himself up over shouldering needed responsibilities, his gut reaming him for thinking this could have gone anywhere, been anything.

He pulled away from the curb with his foot on the gas while he worked to put the brakes on his heart. He'd see her each and every Thursday night, and at fundraising events no doubt, but her reaction to his work constraints added further bricks to her walled-in existence. Right now, Jeff didn't have the time needed to make the climb.

And because he actually liked himself, who he was and what he'd accomplished so far in life, he was pretty sure he shouldn't have to.

Chapter Nine

Hannah's phone rang as she closed up the library a few days later. She fumbled with her keys while juggling the phone and answered just in time, sounding rushed when she wasn't even close to rushed, a sad scenario at age thirty-four. "Hello."

"Is this Hannah Moore?"

Hannah paused, the unfamiliar voice reminding her of intrusive reporters and media hounds relentlessly pursuing a story, only she saw nothing about her Ironwood actions as noteworthy.

"Yes." Caution tainted her tone.

"Hannah, this is Dana Brennan. I volunteered to oversee the food preparations for the Harvest Dinner the library group is holding in conjunction with the Farmer's Fair."

"Jeff's mother."

The other woman's microsecond hesitation said she found it interesting that Hannah classified her that way, which was totally understandable because…

Because Hannah hadn't stopped thinking about Jeff since her rude about-face Sunday morning, making him feel guilty about his job when scores of people depended upon his business. She bit back a sigh of recrimination and covered smoothly. "Jeff mentioned he was going to sign you up for food because, in his words, nobody does it better."

Dana laughed but Hannah was pretty sure the older woman had picked up more than Hannah meant to say with two little words. "What a lovely compliment. And that sounds like my son—hardworking, industrious and appreciative of a good meal."

Hannah had watched him down a twenty-ounce steak at dinner the other night, so she was no stranger to his formidable appetite. "Sounds like the same guy. Do you need help with the dinner planning? There are committee members who'd love to talk with you tomorrow night."

"I've actually got everything planned out," Dana replied, her gentle voice self-assured. "There's a local group of gals who love to put on this sort of thing and we haven't had the chance in a while. If I could come to the meeting and present my plans and ideas for approval, that would be great."

"I'll put you on the agenda when I type it up today and add you to our volunteer list, Mrs. Brennan."

"Oh, Dana, dear, please. If we're going to be working together, first names are so much more fun."

"Dana, then. I'll see you tomorrow night."

"Wonderful."

Hannah headed for home, the crisp October day beautiful, the hillside colors deepening with time.

Her mother's distinctive ringtone interrupted her musings as she neared the apartment. "Hey, Mom. What's up?"

"Just checking in." Jean Moore's voice held warmth and reassurance. She'd obviously been eyeing the calendar, watching the days advance, a family habit every autumn. "How are you doing, honey?"

"I'm doing well, actually," Hannah told her and was surprised by how true that was. "Very well, in fact."

"Hannah, that's wonderful. I'm so happy to hear you say that."

She didn't add "at last," but they both recognized the inference.

"Are you busy with work?"

With work and life, Hannah admitted to herself, another thought of Jeff's quirked grin and bright eyes making her squirm inside since she'd mucked that up. "Yes, we've got a library fundraising project going on that's eating up my spare time and it's been good for me. All around."

"I'm glad, Hannah."

Hannah read her mother's relief and couldn't disagree. "Me, too. Hey, I've got to go. I just got home and there's a package on the step. But first, tell me how adorable this new baby is, our little Caitlyn Jean."

Jean laughed out loud, embracing the new subject matter like any first-time grandma would. "She's precious beyond belief. She's like a mix of you and Leah, absolutely adorable, and Nick is going to be a wonderful father. I can just tell."

"I agree totally," Hannah replied. Her brother Nick's fun, gentle nature was perfect for fatherhood. "And I can't wait to see her, to see all of you. I'm looking forward to Thanksgiving."

"Well…"

The single word said something had gone awry with Nick's well-laid plans. "You're not coming up to Philly for the baptism?"

"We're doing Thanksgiving with John's family this year and it seems rude to head up north right after we've arrived, don't you think? And since we're coming up at Christmas, it gets a little expensive."

And right there was reason enough to hate the long-lasting effects of a broken family. Her stepfather's discomfort around her father dictated her mother's actions, and as wrong as that seemed, Hannah knew better than to expect anything else. "Is it less rude to miss your granddaughter's christening?"

"Unfortunately we don't have limitless funds, travel's expensive and John's pension fund took a huge hit, so we've got to pick and choose. And we'll see you at Christmas if you make the drive to Nick's house in Bucks County."

"I understand." And she did, although a part of Hannah wished they all lived closer. "I'll let you guys know about Christmas. It mostly depends on the weather. Getting caught on I-81 in a blizzard isn't my idea of fun."

"Me neither. And Hannah?"

"Yes?"

"It's nice to hear you sounding so good. So strong."

Her mother's approval added a layer of strength to her growing confidence. "Thanks, Mom. I think so, too."

She pocketed the phone and stared at the box on the stoop, the bold, black marker address way too familiar.

Brian.

She sighed, lifted the box, felt the lightness of it and wondered what on earth he might have sent her at this late date. She'd left nothing of consequence in Illinois, except a good part of her heart and soul, unboxable items she was reclaiming step by step.

Toss it.

The advice seemed timely. No way did Hannah want her growing initiative blindsided by the parcel's contents. She made it halfway around the house, then paused and shifted her gaze up, the bright blue sky edged by an incoming storm system.

Was fear driving her thoughts of dumping the box? Or common sense, a necessary attribute touted by therapy?

"Do not fear what they fear; do not be frightened." Peter's presence in the Bible was brief, a span of two letters, but his encouragement to face fear and bind to courage touched Hannah's heart. Sighing, she took the box inside and pushed it into a closet for another day, another time. Right now, basking in her mother's words of pride, she had no intention of interrupting the current upward cycle.

She'd deal with the box later. The packaged presence was unable to hurt without her tacit permission. But for the moment, setting it aside shielded her from memories that had owned her for too long.

Hannah looked lovely and that seemed so unfair, Jeff thought as he strode into the library Thursday evening, determined to keep everything quick, friendly and business oriented. One look at Hannah in some kind of fitted dress tossed those well-scripted plans out the window.

He'd come early on purpose, wanting to go over a couple of points with her. But when she met his gaze he morphed into a tongue-tied teen boy, captivated by her grace, her charm, the look of her.

She moved his way, seemingly unaware of the war raging within him. So why did he lean forward as she drew near, take a deep, slow breath and sigh, his mouth a whisper's breadth from her cheek? "You smell delightful."

Her answering smile feathered her cheek against his mouth, the sweet softness sublime, but common sense reminded him he'd walked away on Sunday with good reason. Hannah had issues with the constraints of his job, her reaction made that obvious, and his job wasn't about to change. So why did that reason seem to vaporize in her presence?

"Thank you."

"Nice dress."

She smiled and her left hand came up, twisting a thin lock of hair, a habit he'd noticed at each meeting. "If I admit I wore it on purpose, do I gain or lose points?"

"I thought we decided to stop keeping score on Sunday." He leveled a straightforward gaze on her. She released her hair and the spiraled curl sprang forth, turning and dipping its way to her shoulder.

"I was rude on Sunday." She paused, glanced away, then drew her attention back as if deliberately choosing her words.

He didn't note any reluctance to engage face-to-face or the hesitation he'd sensed at previous meetings. Instead she faced him with a look of understanding. "And I didn't mean to be. Sometimes my emotional buttons get pushed by circumstance, triggering out-of-line reactions."

"And my needing to work triggered you?"

"On a Sunday, before watching football," she explained. "Which probably seems ridiculous, but…"

"It reminded you of someone else."

"In part, yes." Her expression said she wasn't proud of her reaction, but understood it.

"And he did quite a number on you."

Her face shadowed. She pursed her lips, the flash of pain in her eyes brief but real. "Life did a number on me, Jeff. Brian's actions just added fuel to the fire."

Brian.

His nemesis had a name. But Jeff had no intention of fighting the past. He'd taken his past on headfirst, moving forward, refusing to let the father's actions shackle the son's choices. Well, until Matt showed up.

Hannah would be wise to do the same.

He stepped back, because the scent and sight of her made him want to help, but he'd learned the hard way that God helped those who helped themselves. It was a belief system he embraced.

"Jeffrey." His mother's voice pulled his attention toward the door. She walked in, her step light, her smile infectious, her warm look taking in the situation at hand. Hannah. Jeff. The mood.

Great.

"Dana, good evening." Hannah moved forward, a hand extended, her surety surprising Jeff. "I'm Hannah Moore, Jeff's cochair."

"Hannah." Dana grasped Hannah's hand and squeezed lightly. "I've heard so much about you."

Hannah worked to keep her voice easy. "All good, I hope."

"Marvelous." Dana squeezed her hand again and shifted her gaze back to Jeff. "I had lunch with Grandma and she's delighted with how quickly you two got things in motion. She's quite impressed, and my mother is not easily impressed."

"That's for sure." Jeff grinned, his manner gilding the words, but Hannah read the distinct difference between the two women now that she'd met both. Martha and Mary, mother and daughter, opposing points of view. The scientist in her said that had to make for interesting holiday conversation and the pacifist within warned those meals should be avoided at all costs. Which wouldn't be a problem because Jeff had shrugged her off, right?

The door swung open and Hannah moved to greet more arriving committee members.

Jeff caught her arm. "May I see you for a minute?"

"Umm…" She glanced from his hand to his face, letting her cool expression speak for her. "You just did."

He flushed slightly. "I was distracted. My bad." He indicated the brightly toned children's area to his right. "For just a moment, Hannah. Please. I wanted your advice on an Advent Walk project before we convene."

"Oh. *Business* talk." She led the way to the children's book nook, then turned and caught him noticing the dress.

That made her smile. The way Jeff managed to stumble over his first words widened it even more. "Listen, I, um…"

"Yes?"

He ran a hand through his hair, the rising voices of the committee members forcing him to speak up. "I was thinking of introducing a buy-a-brick campaign in conjunction with the Advent Walk."

Hannah frowned. "Explain."

"Jamison schedules an Advent Walk every year."

"Right." Hannah drew the word out deliberately. She'd

only been in town a few years, but the quaint tradition of people walking from church to church around the town green, carrying candles for light and greens to decorate the church doors had proven delightful. The gathered group caroled as they walked, and once a church door had been decorated for the Advent season, they paused within that church to pray before proceeding to the next house of worship. The evening concluded with a dessert hour in the newly refurbished youth center, a marvelous finishing touch to a small-town celebration.

"But because there's no sidewalk, we walk in the street."

"We do," she agreed slowly. "But it's not like there's a lot of traffic in the street, Jeff. On a weekend December night."

"But what if we sold pavers to create an Advent walkway for next year?" His animated gaze said he liked the idea, and it was village-centered enough for people to embrace. "I called Winchell Brick and the owner said we could get the pavers at cost and they'd donate the underlayment stone and sand. That way we could build the walk next summer, have a pretty path to do the Advent Walk from that point on and a safe path for kids over the summer when traffic to and from I-86 does get busy."

Hannah recognized the merit in his well-considered plan. "I like the idea," she told him. "And we could sell the stones for a fifty percent profit with the proceeds going to the library fund, staying community-based with a positive outcome as a benefit."

"Exactly."

The grouped tables were rapidly filling with committee members. Hannah headed that way. "It's a great idea, Jeff. Go ahead and introduce it. I've got your back."

She crossed the room to get the meeting started. Her defined movements warred with the undertone of hesitancy he'd witnessed, but he wasn't good at reading hints and signals. He needed straightforward direction.

Hannah threw curves.

His current time constraints might be temporary, but as a company executive and design team leader, they'd resurface as business grew. And he couldn't afford to mess up, not with so much at stake.

"I waited patiently for the Lord. He turned to me and heard my cry."

The psalm mocked Jeff. He'd stopped waiting patiently for anything years ago, needing to be in charge. But right now, watching Hannah's ease with the other committee members, he wondered what he hoped to gain by rushing through life. Did he want his measure of success to be in business only?

"Imagine what my parents thought," his mother exaggerated, amusing the group as he approached, "when they got me instead of the science-loving prototype they envisioned. While my mother devoured every issue of *American Scientist,* I was hiding in my room reading romance novels and practicing the piano, imagining myself a modern-day Elizabeth Bennett."

Hannah laughed with the others, lilting and sweet, the kind of reaction he'd like to inspire. Of course, he was a stuffed shirt scientist, like his grandparents. But Hannah liked science. She'd said so.

Which meant he might still have a chance, although after tonight's fiasco, his opportunities appeared dim.

"Do you still play, Dana?" Miss Dinsmore asked as she settled into a seat, a huff of breath making her sound tired.

"I do." Dana smiled at her old teacher before indicating Jeff with a wave of her hand. "And I forced Jeff and Meredith to learn because as much as I respect the periodic table and great haircuts, the arts and a nice garden are food for the soul. A good life should embrace balance."

Jeff read her message, but wouldn't pursue that now. He called the meeting to order and went through the customary procedural notes before offering his idea up for a vote.

Reverend Hannity raised his hand. "Yes, Reverend?"

"The idea of a walkway is wonderful, Jeff," the reverend exclaimed. "I know the other pastors will offer full support. We've talked about it amongst ourselves, but the village right-of-way made it impossible to do without board permission."

"Can we get permission?" Hannah asked Jeff. "Do we need to attend a board meeting to present the idea?"

He nodded, hearing the word *we* and wondering if she'd deliberately just offered him another night of her time. Most likely not. "They meet on the first and third Wednesdays, so if we can put together a prospectus with Winchell Brick, we could present it to the board next week and get things rolling. This would be a carryover-type fundraiser that we'd work on throughout the winter."

"Who would build the path?" Miss Dinsmore wondered out loud. "Volunteers are fine, but a permanent path needs to be carefully graded."

"We could help with that," Callie offered. "My dad and his crew are great at putting in landscape walls and paths and this is the same idea, just wider and longer. I'll run it by him, but I'm sure he'll say yes."

"Thanks, Callie." Jeff smiled at her, then scanned the group. "Objections?"

No one raised their hand.

He nodded before shifting his attention back to Hannah. "Then we'll approach the town board next week and seek approval contingent on raising the necessary funds by selling the bricks."

He included her on purpose, she was sure of it, and there was no wiggle room when they were surrounded by a room full of people. By the time the other committee members headed home, she'd forgotten the list of reasons why she *shouldn't* accompany Jeff to the meeting.

That meant they'd be together two nights next week, and while a part of her thought of that with anticipation, another part urged caution. She decided to ignore both as she stowed her paperwork and notes in her shoulder bag. Jeff gathered his things in similar fashion and headed her way, a glance at his watch telling her she was taking too much time.

Well, too bad. She'd been walking to her car for three years; she hadn't needed an escort before and didn't need one now.

Jeff glanced at his watch again. Hannah swept him a quick glance. "You don't have to wait for me. I'm fine."

He frowned and looked at her, then the watch, before an "aha" expression brightened his features. "I wasn't in a hurry. My watch seems to have stopped at seven fifty-two."

His watch broke. Suddenly Hannah felt foolish.

He wasn't trying to push her along. Or lamenting the time like Brian had done so often, making her work seem less vital.

"And I was thinking we should get together this weekend," Jeff continued, "to put together an intelligent proposal about the sidewalk fundraiser."

"I know nothing about building sidewalks," Hannah said as she approached the door. "You'd do better to find somebody else."

"We don't have to know the how-tos," Jeff explained, following her outside. "Just the basics. And it would look better to the town board if we both attend the meeting since we're cochairs."

Jeff had a good point. Their old-school town officials might need some convincing, and two was better than one.

"All right."

"Can we get together this Saturday to check out Winchell Brick?" Jeff asked as they crossed the parking lot. "Once we've got sizes and prices figured out we could head to my place or yours, figure out the square footage and the application process and then present the full package to the board. What do you think?"

"I'm here until three."

"And Winchell's closes at four on Saturday," Jeff mused as they reached her car. "How about if I pick you up here and we go straight to Winchell's? I'll let Ted know we're coming and he can advise us."

She couldn't dispute the plan, and since she didn't exactly find spending an evening with Jeff a hardship, that meant they'd be together three of the next six nights. Well. She could keep things together for three evenings. Right?

One glance up into his eyes nixed that assumption.

"We can get takeout and have a working supper," Jeff continued. "Chinese, Italian or pizza."

Hannah smiled. Jamison didn't sport much in the way of Indian, Thai or sushi. "Chinese. From Happy Garden. Because I like the name."

Her answer drew his smile. "Happy Garden, it is." He watched as she climbed into her car, then raised a hand. "I'll see you Saturday. Drive careful."

"I will. The whole three blocks." She offered a quick wave and left him standing as she drove off, mixed feelings vying for her attention.

She wanted to see him. The spark of attraction that burned brighter in his presence felt good.

But she was driving herself crazy trying to read something into his every movement, hunting for signs that made him more or less like Brian, and that wasn't healthy. "Father, help me. You know me, Lord, You know what I've seen. What I've done. You know the cowardly soul that lingers inside. I don't want to be that person anymore, but I don't know how to take full command again. Show me. Please."

You know exactly what you need to do, her conscience retorted. *And until you walk into a school and take your place in front of a classroom again, you let evil win, letting fear stand in your way. You know what needs to be done. You just won't do it.*

Not won't. Can't, thought Hannah. *I* can't *do it. There's a difference.*

But her heart knew there wasn't and while she might be able to turn off the mental scoldings, there was no way to silence her heart. Like it or not, she was a teacher. And a tiny part of her dared to dream of doing it again.

Chapter Ten

Hannah pretended to scowl at a make-believe watch when Jeff rolled to a stop in front of the library entrance at 3:07 p.m. on Saturday. He started to climb out but she hopped in before he had a chance.

"Chivalry later." She buckled her seat belt and shot him a glance. "Clock's ticking."

"I know. I worked this morning and gave the yard one last mowing. At least I'm hoping it's one last mowing, and the cold front headed our way seems to agree. And by the way—" he gave her gold top and dark brown sweater a quick look "—you looked wonderful standing there with the trees turning color behind you."

"Really?" He had no idea how much that compliment meant to her. She beamed. "Thank you."

"You're welcome. Got your notebook?"

"Right here."

"And Ted Winchell knows we're running short on time so he's gathered information for us. And once we're done, we can head to my place if that's okay, eat and outline our presentation?"

"Sounds like a plan." She leaned forward, then paused, one finger ready to hit Play. "Music?"

"Sure."

She hit a switch, heard the music playing and sent him a sideways glance. "VeggieTales? Really?"

He laughed and hit Eject. "Trent and I worked this morning. We had his daughter Cory with us so Alyssa could have time with baby Clay because he was running a fever. Five-year-olds like listening to the same CD over and over again. Kind of like women."

Hannah raised a hand. "Guilty as charged. I have my favorites and Cory Michaels is one smart little girl. And adorable. How Alyssa handles three kids and a full-time job with Trent out of town is a marvel."

"You're right." Jeff pulled into the parking lot abutting Winchell Brick and turned the engine off. "And that realization should be enough to make me feel guilty. I've only had the increased workload at the factory."

"'A man works from sun to sun…'" Hannah started the quote and laughed.

"Yeah, yeah." Jeff sent her a grin as they headed up the walk, sweet and sincere, a smile that faded as soon as he stepped in the door.

"Thanks for all this, Ted." A dark-haired man reached out to shake Ted Winchell's hand. "Hank Marek began this project with solid goals and I want to follow that lead. Having the current prices on materials is crucial."

"Yes, it is." Ted turned, saw Jeff, smiled, gave him a quick "just a moment" hand sign, then turned back. "Matt, if you need anything else, give me a call. I can honor that quote through next spring unless something unforeseen happens in the market. In that case, I'll call you."

"Sounds good."

The dark-haired man turned and spotted Jeff and Hannah at the door. He drew a deep breath and looked ill at ease, his right hand clutching a fistful of papers in an iron grip. "Jeff."

"You're buying the Marek subdivision?" Jeff stepped forward, shoulders taut, wondering why he had to run into Matt right now. "You'd stoop that low?"

"The bank's already taken it over. It's falling into disrepair. So, yes, if I can crunch the numbers, I'm going to buy it and complete it. Until this moment it was a quiet deal—"

"I'm sure of that," Jeff retorted.

Matt continued as if Jeff hadn't spoken. "And because we're at a sensitive part of the negotiations, I'd appreciate you keeping this confidential."

Ted shot Matt a look of chagrin. "I'm sorry, Matt. I should have finished this with you in the office."

Matt shook his head. "My brother understands the art of careful negotiation, Ted. I'm sure he'll respect my wishes."

The word *brother* drew Hannah's attention. Jeff felt her eyes on him, sensed the shift of emotion. And he knew better than to make a public spectacle. Wasn't that exactly why he worked so hard to spit-polish the family name, trying to erase Neal Brennan's high-profile mistakes? But it was a tough go when one of those missteps stood larger than life before him, way too self-assured for an ex-con.

Jeff's mother believed Matt had paid his price by doing eighteen months in juvie.

Katie Bascomb was sentenced to a lifetime with a missing right leg.

Jeff had a hard time seeing justice in that equation, but he ground his jaw and shut his mouth, eager to maintain the family dignity. He'd been doing fine with that until Matt showed up.

He moved to let Matt by, refusing to introduce him to Hannah. As he passed, Matt dipped his chin Hannah's way in a nod of respect. "Ma'am."

She nodded back, then shot Jeff a look that hinted at disappointment.

Her look cut deep. Once again Matt's presence cast him in a bad light.

"Jeff." Ted stepped forward, determined. "I've got your facts and figures back here in my office, but let me show you guys a few ideas first."

"Thank you." Hannah smiled at Ted and extended her hand. "I'm Hannah Moore and I'm helping chair the fund-raising."

"Nice to meet you." Ted shook her hand before leading them to the far wall. "I stopped up in Jamison the other day to examine the existing masonry work on the churches. Fundamentally you can use anything for the path. Aesthetically, I'd go with fieldstone pavers." He pointed to the wall display. "You could go with the pink-tinged or gray-tinged stone. Either would draw together the preexisting aged conditions of the five churches surrounding the round green of the park."

"Could we combine them?" Hannah asked.

Ted grinned. "You've got a good eye. Yes. Either works fine, but blended they'd carry the right color balance. They're made for long-lasting good looks and foot traffic, and with the proper underlayment they won't shift and gap with repeated frost, ice and snow. Sound good?"

"It does." Jeff nodded, determined to focus on the task at hand. He shifted his attention to Hannah, wishing he hadn't caused that guarded look in her eye. "Do you think we need to present the board with various options or go with this one alone?"

"Good question." She scanned the other displays, frowned and shrugged. "Nothing else is exactly right, correct?" She met Ted Winchell's gaze.

He shook his head. "Not in my estimation."

"And you're the resident expert."

He smiled. "Well, I don't like to brag...."

Hannah laughed and waved her hand at the stone they'd chosen. "Let's go in with this. The more decisive we appear, the more confidence we'll inspire."

"I like how you think." Ted led them into the office, typed

a few figures into an existing spreadsheet, then printed the results. "This gives you the information you'll need to present to the board." He handed Hannah a brochure from the stone company. "And this one is the cost of what we're donating."

Jeff looked at the donated figure and whistled. "Ted, that's mighty generous of you guys."

Ted shrugged. "My brother is buried in the graveyard behind Holy Name. My parents got married in Good Shepherd just before Reverend Hannity came. My grandmother still goes to the White Church at the Bend each and every Sunday." He indicated the figures with a nod. "Family takes care of family, right? It was the least we could do."

His words stifled Jeff's reply, and Hannah stepped into the silence.

"Thank you."

"You're welcome. And good luck," he told them as he walked them to the door, his keys in hand. "Between Councilman Bascomb and Councilwoman Jackson, you might have your work cut out for you. They pretty much say no to everything, and that leaves Cyrus as the tiebreaker, and Cyrus can't make a decision to save his life."

"You're kidding, right?" Hannah scanned Ted's face, then turned to Jeff. "Please tell me he's kidding."

"I wish I could."

"So we did all this and they're going to say no? What was the point?"

Jeff exchanged looks with Ted. "Because we're going to schmooze them into saying yes."

"More games?"

"Let's call it strategic planning," Ted told her. He exchanged a frank look with Jeff before returning his attention to Hannah. "Small towns have advantages and disadvantages. An advantage is knowing everyone because there is no such thing as hiding in a small town. So you play to the council's sensitivities to win their individual votes."

"And the disadvantage is?" Hannah arched a brow.

He shrugged and laughed. "Secrets don't really exist. No one comes here to hide because everything's an open book. And no council member is going to want the smudge of being the one person to vote down a good thing for the town because that's political suicide."

She pointed a finger at Jeff. "You got me into this on purpose, didn't you?"

"Absolutely. I wasn't about to take them on alone, Hannah. I'm brave, but I'm not stupid."

His words brought his confrontation with Matt back to mind. He hadn't been brave then. He'd been contentious and ornery, both of which equaled stupid.

And he'd done it in front of Hannah and Ted, after he promised himself he'd get a handle on these feelings about Matt.

Hannah's quiet look of appraisal said he'd lost points, which was fine, wasn't it?

Define fine, his conscience niggled. *And get a grip.*

Easier said than done.

Saint Peter's question popped into his mind again. *"How many times must I forgive my brother, Lord? Seven?"*

Jeff knew Christ's answer. He understood the severity behind the response, the virtually limitless cache of forgiveness. Now he just had to find the strength to go along with the understanding.

"Jeff, this is lovely." Hannah surveyed the stately Colonial from the driveway a half hour later as the late-day light danced beams across the west-facing house. She turned to face Jeff, her right hand indicating the house and the yard. "This is yours?"

"You like it?"

"Try love it. Is it as sweet inside?"

"Let's find out." He grinned and lifted the two bags of

takeout. "Since it appears I'll be eating leftover Chinese for a week, we might as well start putting a dent in this."

"I told you not to get the cashew chicken or the sesame shrimp," she scolded as they reached the front door. "Just because I said I liked them didn't mean we needed four entrées."

"I enjoy choices, and I lived through many a college weekend on cold Chinese," he told her. "So I actually like having leftovers in the fridge."

"You surprise me."

"How's that?"

Hannah shrugged. "You live in a big house you probably rarely see and you eat cold Chinese out of paper cartons."

"The house was a wise investment about seven years ago when prices were down and the former owners moved south. The Chinese food, well, I like cold Chinese."

"It's beautiful, Jeff." Hannah turned in a slow circle once inside, taking in the entry hall, the oak-trimmed rooms embracing the foyer and the staircase before her, a nod to older times and more stately bearings. "And what a staircase."

Jeff grinned boyishly. "That's what sold me. I could just see me as a kid, sliding down that banister, listening to my mother scold me."

"Having met your mother, I can't imagine she scolded too loud or too long. She's sweet and gentle."

"Unlike me?"

Hannah heard an almost plaintive note in his voice. "I think life might have handed you a two-sided coin and you're not too sure how to handle that."

"You mean that scene with my brother."

She made a little face. "Your business. Not mine."

He crossed the large and fairly empty dining room and entered a big, homey kitchen. Hannah followed, appreciating the welcoming stature of the elegant old rooms. The inviting maple table and chairs said the kitchen was his room of preference. He set the bags on the kitchen table and indicated them with a wave as he withdrew plates from ivory-stained cupboards. "Buying beef, shrimp, chicken and lo mein should be considered at least a little sweet."

"Since food is a necessity, and I've witnessed your confession about loving leftovers, I'm afraid buying too much doesn't measure up."

"How about this?" He handed her the plates, opened the fridge and withdrew a string-tied white box. He slit the string, lifted the cover and withdrew a chocolate enhanced cannoli. "When it comes to desserts, I like Italian best." He held the pastry to her mouth and Hannah bit down carefully, letting the mingled tastes of dark chocolate, crisp cookie and sweet filling meld before she swallowed.

"Amazing. Gimme." She took the cannoli from his hand, took another bite and laughed at his look of chagrin as she began opening bags one-handed.

She fit, Jeff decided, seeing her there in front of the charming glass-fronted kitchen cabinets surrounding the kitchen on three sides. Her long braid dipped and swung with her movements, fetching atop the gold knit turtleneck beneath a dark brown nubby sweater. He grabbed silverware from a drawer, then plunked them onto the table with a deliberate lack of finesse. "Casual okay?"

She laughed, licked the last tidbit of cannoli cream from her fingers and agreed. "I love casual."

So did he. The smidge of pretentiousness that sometimes accompanied his job annoyed him. Over the years he'd dated a few women who fawned over that aspect of his career.

Not Hannah. She filled a trucker-size plate from the various cartons and then nailed him with a scathing look when he scanned the plate. "I do believe we've already had this discussion. I like to eat."

"I remember. You just surprise me because most women

pretend they don't eat, then wolf down a bag of chips when they get home because they're starving."

"And you know this because?"

"I have a sister."

"Meredith." Hannah nodded, pulled out a chair and took a seat. "And Megan says she gives great haircuts. That's an art right there."

"You're not thinking of cutting your hair, are you?" It was no concern of his, but the very idea sat wrong with Jeff. In an age when so many women went short and sassy, he loved Hannah's long, tumbling curls. Today's braid just reminded him that braids could be undone.

"Maybe. Why?"

He kept his tone neutral with effort. "Your hair is beautiful, Hannah. It's perfect."

Surprise and pleasure infused her cheeks with color, but he was pretty sure she veered from serious talk for the same reasons he did, because this could never work. "Well, thank you, Jeff. I like your hair, too."

She was laughing at him. Oh, not out loud, she was too nice for that, but inside? Yeah, he was sure of it. But he'd been around the block often enough to know how far he could bend without breaking.

He sent her an easy grin over the paper cartons, gripped her fingers lightly and tried not to think of how cool and soft her skin felt as he said grace.

"Done." Hannah settled the last carton into the refrigerator. "Would you mind if we take a quick walk around the neighborhood? Otherwise I might fall asleep while you factor stones and dimensions."

Jeff grabbed her jacket and his. "Works for me. Our days of nice weather are dwindling."

"That's for sure." Hannah fastened her coat, stepped outside and drew in a deep breath. "But this is wonderful, isn't it? What a great neighborhood you live in. All these old homes. The trees. The streetlights. Positively poetic."

"You like poetry, Hannah?"

"Doesn't everyone?" She read his expression and burst out laughing. "Guess not. I expect your mother had a time with you, trying to balance your quest for scientific exploration with 'Twinkle, Twinkle, Little Star' on the keyboard."

"I didn't make it easy for her," Jeff admitted. He kicked a tiny stone off the sidewalk and watched it skitter away. "I love trying new things. Reinventing the wheel. I had a hard time understanding why she wanted me to do things I wasn't naturally good at while messing with the time I wanted to devote to what I liked."

"Because variety *is* important." Hannah eyed the starlit sky between gold-tinged maple boughs; the changing color intensified with each passing day. "And a parent's job as primary educator is to create that balance because they have an adult vantage point."

"You're a teacher."

He studied her, surprised. She pulled in a breath and fought a wince. "Yes."

"What did you teach?"

"High school science."

"Ah." He nodded, appeased. "I wondered why scientific jargon slipped into your speech so easily. I expect you were good."

Her face showed mixed emotion. "It was a long time ago. I like what I do now. It's peaceful."

"But is it exciting?" Jeff wondered out loud.

Hannah shook her head. "No, and that's just another reason to love it."

He accepted her words, as if it was the most natural thing in the world for a science teacher to be working part-time in a hamlet-sized library. Should he ask why she stopped?

Her expression told him to hold back.

He had time, as far as he knew. Now what he needed was patience, and that had been on his mother's prayer list for decades. Walking with Hannah? Talking with her? Getting to know the woman within?

That was worth every patient moment he could muster.

Chapter Eleven

No way could he wait until Wednesday night's board meeting to see Hannah again. The fact that this was his first thought on a bleak Sunday morning made Jeff take notice.

He called her cell phone but when his call went directly to voice mail, he realized her phone was either off or uncharged. He left a message, got cleaned up and headed toward Jamison for church, not even trying to pretend he wasn't hoping to see her. Maybe grab that breakfast she'd offered the week before. He headed over to Holy Name, slipped into the back of the old stone church and realized it was rock-band Sunday when the pounding of drums nearly pierced his ears.

Then Hannah slipped into the pew beside him.

"You're late," he whispered, refusing to disguise his pleasure.

She shook her head. "Nah, I'm not. I went to Good Shepherd to sit with you and avoid the first-Sunday-of-the-month amplifiers over here. But then I saw you racing up the steps…"

"Running a touch behind," he admitted, wondering if she knew how perfectly her mottled blue scarf matched her eyes. "So you came over here to join me? Without earplugs?"

Her answering smile said enough. The way she turned her

attention to the altar meant she didn't dare pursue this line of conversation at this moment.

Which only meant there'd be another time and another place, and Jeff was okay with that.

"Breakfast?" he asked as they headed down the church steps later, his ears reverberating from the church's less than perfect acoustics. "My treat."

Her bright smile encouraged him to edge closer, but she shook her head, regretful. "Not today. I've got a gazillion things to catch up on, and I promised myself I'd do them today because we have the Wednesday night council meeting, the Thursday night fundraising meeting and next weekend is the Farmer's Fair and Harvest Dinner. I'm swamped."

"I'll help."

"With my laundry? Umm...no."

He laughed. "Then I'll help with other stuff. If we work together we can spend the later part of the day doing something fun."

"You don't have anything to do today?"

Her words reminded him of last Sunday's debacle, but he wouldn't lie to her. "I've got contract bids I need to go over, but I don't want a repeat of last week."

"And it's football season."

"So?" He paused at her car, watched as she unlocked the door and then offered a solution. "You go home and do your laundry and whatever else you need to get done. I'll go over my contracts and pick you up around two."

"Make it four."

He shook his head. "Too late and too long to wait." Color invaded her cheeks at his words and he smiled, grazing a finger against the flushed skin. "Three. And that's four hours longer than I care for."

Her gaze melted. She squared her shoulders, trying to look businesslike, but from the occasional looks Jeff intercepted from passersby, no one mistook their conversation for library business. "Three o'clock. I'll pick you up. Wear jeans."

"Bossy."

Her pleased smile softened the crisp response. He pushed her door closed, leaned down and grinned, giving her mouth a look of longing that seemed to deepen her expression. He nodded, letting his appreciative look speak for him. "See you then."

Jeff Brennan managed to put her in a tailspin with a simple look, a gentle smile, despite her best efforts to keep him at bay.

Keep him at bay? You ran over to Holy Name the minute you caught sight of him. That's not exactly maintaining an arm's length.

Hannah pressed cool hands against her warm cheeks as she decided she was not sick, just flustered.

It was delightful.

But also scary.

You will not dredge up fear and foreboding. Weren't you listening this morning, hearing Isaiah's words? "Do not be afraid. I am with you always. Follow me, and I will give you rest."

Hannah settled laundry into various drawers and took a clutch of hangers to the closet. She withdrew several summery tops with one hand and refilled the spot with long-sleeved blouses and turtlenecks. Her toe caught the box she'd stuffed in there, edging it forward. The closet floor was too shaded to see Brian's bold, black script, but she didn't need a visual to picture the slanted *H* and *M,* evidence of Brian's decisive flair.

Open it.

Not today. Today she was outdistancing the past by embracing the future. No matter what might come of this attraction to Jeff Brennan, wallowing in the past was no longer an option.

She finished stowing things away and barely had enough time to brush her teeth and fluff her hair before her doorbell rang at two-fifty. She strode to the door and yanked it open. "You're early."

He grinned and unlatched the screen door. "Couldn't wait any longer."

His words lifted her heart, soothed her soul. The feeling of being cared for was one of God's most natural highs. She waved him in, scurried into the bathroom for a hair clip and scolded, "Do you know how much a girl can get done in ten minutes, Jeff?"

He laughed from the living room and shot back, "Considering the girl's God-given beauty, there's little that needs doing."

So sweet of him to say so. She clipped back her hair, touched up her mascara and rejoined him in the front room. He gave her an appreciative smile, then motioned to Nick's family photo on the bookshelf. "This wasn't here a few weeks ago."

Add great powers of observation to his list of many talents, Hannah decided. "My brother Nick, his wife, Leah, and their brand-new baby girl, Caitlyn Jean. I've got the honor of being her godmother on Thanksgiving weekend."

Jeff traced the baby's face with one blunt finger, the gentle action sweet beyond words. "She's beautiful."

Hannah smiled. "She is. My mom says she looks like a combination of Leah and me."

Jeff eyed the photo, tilted it, examining the baby's profile. Then he frowned and shook his head, humor glinting in his eyes. "You drool more."

"Stop." Hannah snatched the picture out of his hands. She waved to her jeans, turtleneck and thick, fleeced hoodie. "Is this good for whatever we're doing?"

"Perfect. Let's go."

"What *are* we doing?" she asked as they headed down the porch steps.

His car wasn't there. Instead he opened the door of a pickup truck that had seen better days. "We're driving this?"

He grinned. "Yup."

"But…"

"In." He waved a hand, then pretended to wince as she clutched his shoulder to climb up. "Nice grip, Han."

She waved his complaint away as he climbed in the driver's side. "What's the plan?"

"You'll see."

A surprise. Hannah had been alive long enough to know that surprises could either enchant or disappoint, but the gleam in Jeff's eye said this one should be fun. And when they pulled up to Breckenridge Farm a few minutes later, she was sure of it.

"Okay." Jeff looked around, puzzled, then waved a hand to the gorgeous fall displays and Hannah. "Pick."

"Pick what?"

"I don't know. Stuff. We're going to decorate our porches for harvest season. It's one of the things we do down here before the Farmer's Fair. Your landlord won't care, will she?"

"No."

"Good. It's silly to have unfestive porches, right? Down-right unpatriotic."

"I couldn't agree more. Where do we start?"

"Straw," Jeff decided. He walked to a stack and removed four bales of straw and stacked them in the back of the pickup.

"And cornstalks for the pillars," Hannah told him. She moved to a huge tepee-style display and handed Jeff eight bunches of cornstalks.

"You don't think this is too many?" he asked, stretching his neck around the cumbersome bundles to see her.

"You have four pillars. I have four pillars. We both have lampposts, and you have that cute decorative fence by the front sidewalk. You can't decorate your porch without carrying the theme throughout."

"Far be it from me to mess with a theme." He hauled the bundled cornstalks into the bed of the truck. "And now pumpkins."

"And squash."

"I love squash," he told her as they lined up an assortment of pumpkins, then balanced the effect with a mix of squashes. "Butternut is my favorite."

"Mine, too." She smiled up at him, the thought of sharing a favorite squash far more pleasant than it should have been. "I like it with brown sugar and butter. And lots of cinnamon."

"I'm getting hungry just thinking about it." He eyed their stash and shook his head. "Something's missing."

"Whimsy."

"Say what?"

Hannah waved toward the far side of the quaint, aged barn. "Fanciful. Fun." She led him to a shed display of scarecrows and birdhouses surrounded by seasonally toned ribbons in nylon and raffia. "I think for your house we should get him." She pointed to a funny-faced scarecrow on a stick, perfect for posing in the hay, his blue jeans topped by red hunter plaid. A bright yellow hat completed the straw man's ensemble.

"And she would look great on my porch," Hannah explained, withdrawing a slightly stout straw woman in a blue flowered dress, her dark green hat embellished with fall-toned flowers.

"Why can't she stay on my porch?" asked Jeff. "They could keep each other company."

Hannah leaned close, whispering the obvious. "They're not married."

It was an innocent bit of teasing, so why did he turn her

way, his expression all sweet and serious, as if the fate of two wooden stick scarecrows meant something?

Hannah swallowed hard. Jeff's questioning look pushed common sense and fear aside.

"I know a preacher." Jeff matched her soft tone as he moved closer, his gaze roaming her face until it settled on her lips. "Several, in fact."

"Do you?" She read the question in his eyes and couldn't pretend she wasn't thinking the exact same thing. She raised one hand and traced his face, his jaw, the sandpaper feel ruggedly male beneath her fingers.

Jeff slipped an arm around her waist, waiting for her to object or duck away, but that was the last thing Hannah wanted to do, although she knew she should. She puffed a breath, a tiny sigh that made him smile and draw her closer before he slanted his mouth over hers, the gentle pressure of his mouth, his embrace, like a wanderer finding home.

The strength of his hands, the stubble of late-day skin, the scent of him, all fresh air and hay with a hint of coffee. Standing there in the privacy of the rustic shed, with Jeff's lips on hers, it was almost easy to think about things like preachers and weddings.

For the scarecrows, that is.

Hannah drew back, ending the kiss, but she trailed a finger of contentment along his cheek, his chin, before indicating the straw woman with a quick look. "What if those two want a big wedding? Neither one of us has time to plan that."

Jeff smiled at her. "Then we find people to help. Did you pick out enough ribbon?"

"This, this and this." She piled the rolls into their woven basket, then glanced around, satisfied. "We did well."

Jeff sent her mouth a teasing glance. "Very well."

Her blush deepened his smile. He grabbed his scarecrow and hers, then headed toward the huge apple display. "Except for apples."

"Apples on the porch?" She frowned and shook her head. "They'll go bad."

"Apples to eat," Jeff told her. He grabbed a half peck of Honeycrisps as they headed inside to pay for their truckful of autumn fun. "And an apple pie for dessert."

"I love apple pie."

Kim Breckenridge added a fresh-baked pie to the basket, then swept them a quick look of question. "Anything else?"

Hannah nudged Jeff. "Cider."

"Great idea."

"A half gallon or whole?"

Jeff eyed the whole gallon and shook his head. "Half. We don't want it to sour and we can always come back for more."

"Which makes my entire family very happy," Kim told him, grinning. She withdrew the cider from an adjacent cooler. "There we go. All set now?"

Jeff eyed the pickup truck and the various things they had on the counter and gulped as he handed over his debit card. "Yes. Please."

He rearranged the truck bed to accommodate the vegetables and straw people while Hannah packed the front seat with food. She settled back into her seat as he shut the tailgate, wondering when she'd last had this much fun.

Maybe never, she decided, smiling as Jeff shifted the peck of apples to make room. She leaned across the front seat and surprised him with a kiss, just a little kiss, a feathering of her mouth against his somewhat grizzled skin. He smiled his thanks, his expression saying more than should be possible with the short weeks they'd known each other. But Hannah read the look in his eyes, the warmth, the caring, the invitation to travel a new path. And for the first time in nearly five years, she felt strong enough to take the chance.

"Oh, Jeff, I love it!"

Since Hannah rarely got this excited about anything, Jeff

enjoyed hearing the uplift in her voice when they finished her porch in the lamplight that evening. He stood back, surveyed the effect, and nodded, pleased that she'd enjoyed the afternoon. "It looks good."

"It looks great," she corrected him. She crossed the porch, then indicated the house with a wave. "Do you want to order a pizza and watch the beginning of the Sunday night game here?"

Jeff digested the invitation. She'd gotten weirded out last week by his work and football. Sure, she'd apologized, but no way was he about to mess with a great afternoon by chancing a bad evening. "Pizza's good, but I've got an early morning and unless I'm really into the team, I don't do late games."

"Pizza it is." She withdrew her phone, hit a number on her speed dial and placed the order. "I'm having them deliver it so we can tip the driver."

"Because?"

"It's Callie's cousin. He usually does construction but with the slowdown he hasn't had much work, so he's going to trade school for electricians and delivering pizzas at night."

Add kind and thoughtful to her growing list of wonderful attributes. She worked two jobs and drove a low-end car, but was willing to shell out five dollars she didn't have to help a young man's dream.

When the doorbell rang, Jeff moved quicker and waved her off. "I've got it."

"But you paid for all the stuff this afternoon," she protested, her chin thrust up in a really cute pout.

Jeff paid the young man, added a considerable tip and a nod of thanks, then turned. "My day, my decision. What kind of guy takes a girl out and makes her pay?"

She smiled, unwilling to argue that. "The worst. Thank you, Jeff." She surveyed the decorated porch and lifted one shoulder. "I'll smile every time I see that porch. Or think of it."

"Perfect."

A part of him longed to jump into hyperdrive, a typical Jeff Brennan move. The wiser portion urged him to pay close attention to laying a foundation of trust, the brick and mortar of a good base. Watching her devour a hefty share of the pizza, he waved outdoors. "Are you intent on making me walk off supper tonight, too? Because the rain just started and I didn't bring an umbrella."

"I have umbrellas, but no. I think we should just sit here with the curtains open and enjoy the fruits of our labors—"

"Vegetables, in this case," he interrupted, smiling.

She accepted his correction, looking really pretty and serious. "*Vegetables* of our labors and spit-polish our presentation."

"Gotcha." Jeff stood and cleaned up the paper plates and napkins, then reached down and hauled her to her feet. "Since we did our civic duty by improving the appearance of both Wellsville and Jamison with great-looking porches, I suppose work is in order."

"I concur." She moved across the room and drew open the drapes, the front porch light showcasing the fall array. "And if we sit here, we can enjoy the view."

"I already am."

She flushed, embarrassed and charmed, her beautiful smile a gift he hadn't expected and probably didn't deserve, but that only made him want to be more deserving.

His mother kept telling him to forgive and forget. To leave the past alone.

He thought he'd done that, but Matt's reappearance proved him wrong. Jeff followed Hannah across the room, took a seat and wondered if he had what it took to make things right. Go the distance. Be the peacemaker his mother and grandmother wanted him to be.

"Blessed are the peacemakers, for they shall be called the children of God." He'd learned that as a child, not under-

standing the depth of its meaning. Now, as Hannah leaned over the projected notes, her fall of hair curtaining half of her face, he understood the import more fully. He was letting his past dictate his present. Was that Matt Cavanaugh's fault?

Hardly.

But Matt had wreaked havoc back in the day, ruining lives in the process.

"I've lost you, I see."

Jeff pushed the puzzle of his life off to the side. "Only temporarily."

"Thinking of work?" She tipped him a look before noting the clock. "If you need to go home and get things done, I can finish this. We're almost done, anyway."

"Not work," he admitted, taking his time. He glanced away, then back. "Family stuff."

"Ah." Hannah sat back, steepled her fingers and met his gaze. "Meeting your brother yesterday."

"*Half* brother."

She considered his words then leaned forward. "I think you've nailed a big part of the problem right there. My parents divorced when I was nine years old. Both remarried. My father never had more kids, but my mother did." She indicated the picture of Nick on the small table beyond Jeff. "And I've never in my life thought of him as a half brother."

"But you lived with him, right?"

"Part of the time. But that's just geography, Jeff."

Jeff didn't want to concede that. "You knew him since he was a baby."

"Yes. But even if I hadn't—" she met his look, determined "—he'd still be my brother. I don't do halfway, Jeff. Ever."

Her words speared him.

He'd have thought the same about himself, but right now he wasn't too sure. Maybe he went full tilt when he had control, and pulled back when uncertainty loomed. Either way, he wasn't a big fan of this conversation. "So. For Wednesday. Do you have time to do a volunteer time chart?"

Did his quick shift back into business mode put that shadow on her face? He thought so. She bent her head, made a few marginal notes and put together a packet of information for him. "I can if you manage to put this into a semblance of order for us."

"I'd be glad to." He stood, wishing they'd never brought up family, wishing…

"Then I'll meet you at the Community Center. Is six-thirty good?"

"Yes."

"Perfect."

"Hannah, I—"

"I loved the decorating." She smiled toward the front porch as she led the way to the door. "And the pizza. Thank you."

He wanted to say more, but good sense told him to hold off. He shrugged into his jacket. "You're welcome. See you Wednesday."

"Yes."

And that was it. He strode across the porch, remembering how carefree she'd looked as they decorated, the innocence of the day reflected in her face, her emotions. The memory of that kiss made him think all kinds of things.

Right up until they started talking about family and she realized he was a jerk of the highest proportions.

Maybe he was, maybe he wasn't, but most days were too chock-full of work to dwell on things like old wrongs.

But you do, his conscience reminded him. *Your quest for bigger, better, stronger is nothing more than trying to best your father. Get over it, already.*

Easier said than done when his life echoed with constant reminders. But whose fault was that? Hadn't he deliberately chosen a similar career to prove to himself and the world that he could do it better?

He headed home, tired and a little miffed that Hannah didn't quite get it. His conscience took great delight in reminding him that the problem probably wasn't Hannah's at all, and that just made him feel worse.

Chapter Twelve

Hannah drew her lightweight jacket snug as she hurried into the Jamison Community Center on Wednesday evening, the sudden dip in temperature a chill reminder. She spotted Jeff and headed his way. "Have you seen the weekend forecast?"

He gave her one of those steady, long looks and quipped back, "Hi, Jeff. How are you tonight? How was your day? Oh, and by the way, have you seen the forecast?"

"Sorry. I'm in business mode. First things first. We've got this nailed—" she held her presentation folder aloft "—and I'm projecting ahead. The weekend forecast is dire and we're putting a lot of stock into this big opening fundraiser. Are we going to bomb?"

"We're hardy stock here, Hannah." Jeff shrugged off her concerns. "A little rain's nothing to get steamed up over."

"We're not talking scattered showers," she retorted. "We're talking monsoons. Flood watches. The real deal."

He still didn't have the decency to look worried. "Everything moves inside the high school if it storms. The performers use the auditorium and we move the dinner to the high school cafeteria."

The high school. Hannah hadn't bargained on that, hadn't given it a thought, actually. His words sent an adrenaline shot to her heart. She had to work to find her voice and when she did, she hoped it didn't tremble. "Where do the vendors set up?"

"Along the hallways," he explained. "It gets a little crowded and the fire marshal turns a blind eye for those two days, but it's doable. And Megan's got a candy booth and a cookie booth this year, so you'll have your hands full between those and the library fundraising booth. You've never driven down for the Fair before?"

Hannah refused to explain that she avoided anything to do with fall or schools, that this was the first time she'd actually felt somewhat normal watching the march of color enrobe the surrounding hillsides. "No. Megan only did one booth in the past, so she didn't need me."

Her excuse was partially true. She was doing better, but the thought of being closed in in the high school during a rainstorm iced her from within, a condition that had nothing to do with external temperatures and everything to do with one young man's murderous rampage. "When do they decide?"

"Friday. If the forecast seems extreme, we go for the indoor venue. How's your scarecrow lady doing? You might want to consider giving her a raincoat for the weekend."

Yes. Concentrate on funny. Sweet. Mundane. Do not think about the high school, do not perseverate, do not allow the past to ruin the present. "The Lord is my light and my salvation; whom should I fear?"

That psalm verse was inscribed on a wooden plaque over her bed and the words engraved on her heart. But despite her push forward, the thought of being entombed in that high school for hours on end blindsided her.

Then it's high time it didn't, her inner voice scolded. *You will be surrounded by people you've come to know and care for. One, especially.*

"Hannah, you there?"

She flushed, painful emotions rising within. "Yes, just thinking of how to do this and make it the best possible experience for all."

"Which for me, just means you're there." Hannah flushed. "Are you hungry?" he asked as the town clerk opened the meeting room door, allowing them to enter. "We could grab something after the meeting."

She shook her head, the idea of food a worst-case scenario right now. "I can't, thanks. I've got to stay ahead of things this week because I'll be working the Fair the whole weekend. I've got the library hours covered, but that means having everything organized for the gal who's stepping in for me."

"Understandable," he agreed. "And since we'll have you trapped indoors, you'll be fairly inaccessible this weekend."

Trapped indoors.

Her heart clenched; the common phrase was uncommonly chilling.

Jeff touched her arm, slowing her progress, letting others move into the room before them. "You okay?"

"Fine." She wasn't. She was about as far from okay as she could get, but she hoped, no, *prayed* it wouldn't show, that she could present a normal face to the world. And right now the world was Jeff Brennan.

King David had wondered out loud what could mortal man do to him, what should he fear?

Hannah had seen what mortal men did firsthand; she'd watched, listened and smelled the horrible aftereffects of man's depravity. And yes, she feared, that was painfully obvious when the prospect of being in a totally unrelated high school during a rained-out festival messed with her emotions.

But she'd grown strong enough now to regain control. Heading into the meeting room, she was determined to push through the wall of sensations steamrolling her. It was a building, no more, no less.

And she was so much better now.

* * *

Bright blue morning sky provided a backdrop for the riot of fall colors surrounding the high school. Hannah parked her car and headed inside, then turned in surprise. Her red car had become silver, and it was newer. Longer. She frowned, waved to a colleague and ducked into the teachers' entrance at ground level, the familiar hallways her home away from home.

As she reached the third level, a voice called her name. She looked around but saw no one, the hall empty and dark as if maintenance forgot to switch the lights on.

She unlocked her classroom door and opened it.

Ten faces looked up at her, expectant.

She frowned and glanced at her watch, but she wasn't wearing a watch. She moved into the room as dark clouds blotted out the sun beyond the long bank of windows; the predicted midday storm arrived early.

Except it wasn't early. The wall clock said 12:32, which meant she was late. Very late. She did an about-face, confused. Then she hurried to her desk as the silent class watched her. Waiting. Wondering. She had to say something, apologize for keeping them waiting. It was unspeakably rude behavior and she was never late for anything. Or rude.

The clouds opened up beyond the glass wall, unleashing a torrent of rain, the dismal sight and sound dulling the day in shaded grays.

She never heard the first gunshot. She was sure of that. Maybe the thunder blotted the noise, masking it.

But she didn't miss one scream, one plea for help as the kids in the adjacent lab room begged for their lives.

She ran for the adjoining door. When she got to it, she didn't open it, fearlessly running in to save the day.

She locked it, using the set of keys clutched in her hand, saving herself and the ten students in her room, but sealing off a possible avenue of escape for nine others.

Their screams echoed as she locked the hallway door, their pleas lost in a volley of gunfire, breaking glass and pouring rain, a cacophony of blended sounds. She scurried, gathering her ten students like baby chicks beneath a falcon's shadow, huddling them behind the half-wall bookcase in front of the windows, while chaos reigned in the lab next door, the eventual silence more formidable than the noise ever thought of being.

Hannah struggled awake, fighting her way out of the dream, clawing through blankets to escape. It took long seconds to realize she'd been dreaming, a dream she hadn't had in over a year.

She sat up, cradling a pillow, wanting to cry, longing to turn back the clock and think of something she could have done other than turn that key.

Many labeled her a hero in the aftermath. That made her sick to her stomach. She was no hero. No matter what she did, she couldn't forget how she used those keys in her hand to lock out three crazed killers, one innocent lab instructor and nine innocent kids.

God forgive her, she'd turned that key, barricaded the door with the help of two sturdy boys, gathered the ten kids in her charge and crouched like a frightened rabbit behind a make-shift bookcase blockade while gunfire shattered the windows above them, showering them in a volley of crushed glass and cold, teeming rain.

Sure, she'd saved some, and everyone told her she should focus on that. Grab the positive and avoid the negative. Scientifically speaking, she understood their reasoning.

But she couldn't forget that *she* was Brad Duquette's intended target, the one he came gunning for because she'd turned down his application for her elite science class. He'd reminded her as he targeted the teacher and students in the adjacent lab, counting them off nice and loud for her benefit.

Dark thoughts invaded her heart, her soul, the memories of so much lost in so little time.

"Father, help me. Be my strength, my heart, feed my soul. Shelter me from this mayhem, from these memories, from this fear. Strengthen me, uphold me, uplift me."

Lisa had told her that life would trigger strong emotional reactions sometimes, that she'd have to bolster herself to push through. "And each time you do, you'll gain strength and momentum," the young therapist promised. "But you need to take it step by step."

The impending weekend loomed before her, the thought of rain beating on the school roof, darkening the windows, weighing heavy.

Because you're letting it, her conscience scolded. *It's rain, nothing more, nothing less, in a building that's common to every community in the world. A school. Go. Do good work. Be at peace.*

Could she?

Hannah clutched the pillow tighter and sighed.

She had to. She knew that. Eyeing the clock she noted the predawn hour and climbed out of bed, knowing there'd be no more sleep this night, praying she wouldn't repeat this performance every night this week in anticipation of the indoor setting.

But if she did?

She would not cave. Not ever again. She'd move forward. No more would she let fear and guilt dog her steps or impede her way. She was determined to take charge of her life, once and for all.

She washed her face, made coffee, opened her laptop and sat down to do something she should have done long ago: write notes of apology to those families whose children died that day, seeking their forgiveness. She hunted through files, found most of their addresses and withdrew a pad of notepaper from her desk drawer.

She'd felt better after talking to Jane Dinsmore about Ironwood, and while she hated what she felt compelled to say to these parents, she knew she had no choice. With God as her witness, she needed to face the enormity of her guilt head-on. And it was high time she did just that.

"I'd prefer snow," Megan grumbled as she and Hannah removed wet, protective plastic sheeting from the stacks of cookies on Saturday morning. "At least snow can be brushed off. This—" she held out a dripping sheet of plastic and shook her head as she glared toward the windows "—borders on ridiculous."

Hannah handed over a fresh roll of paper towels. "Don't talk. Wipe. We need to get set up down the hall and some bossy gray-haired man is standing guard at the hall door to make sure we don't mess up his floors."

"Ray Bernard, head custodian. And believe me—" Meg leaned closer "—I wouldn't have the nerve to mess up his floors." She looked up and her smile broadened. "And what a coincidence, Jeff Brennan just happens to be coming this way. In all the years I've been manning the Farmer's Fair, I don't recall seeing Jeff this early or this excited."

"Stop." Hannah met his gaze and knew their mutual reaction was ill-hidden.

"You made it." Jeff didn't even pause, just grabbed Hannah's hand and swept a quick kiss to her mouth before offering his help, as if kissing her in public was the most natural thing in the world. He squeezed her hand, hefted multiple boxes of cookies onto a dry cafeteria cart and led Hannah past the grim-faced custodial sentry and down the hall. "They put the cookie booth down here and tucked the fudge tables in the clump of food booths just beyond the gym." He withdrew a floor plan from his pocket and marked her spot with an X before handing it over.

"A cheat sheet. Excellent."

He nodded as he shifted the boxes aside to make room for a volunteer lugging the rest from the kitchen. "Thanks, Cheryl. And yeah, the cheat sheets are a must because a lot of the vendors don't know their way around the high school and it's easy to get yourself turned around."

"Thank you, Jeff."

"You're welcome." His gaze lingered on her face, her eyes, as if wondering... What? What was he thinking? She had no idea, but the look disappeared as someone called his name from down the hall. "I'm in and out today with stuff going on at the plant. The library fundraiser booth is near the front, but if you need me for anything—" he moved closer, his gentle expression a promise "—just call me, okay?"

Hannah drew a deep breath, refusing to look around, not wanting to see the lockers, bulletin boards and trophy cases. Today her eyes would face straight ahead or be trained on cookies. She swept the stack of boxes a look. "By the time I get set up here, people will be coming in droves, keeping me so busy I won't have a spare minute to think of you."

He cupped her cheek with one broad hand, his gentle look strengthening her. "I hope that's not true."

She flushed, saw his grin and felt like her world edged a little more upright. "Go. We've got work to do."

"See you later."

Her heart skipped a beat at that thought, the simple phrase a blessed promise. And just like she'd assured Jeff, by the time she got the booth festooned with harvest plaid table-cloths, Indian corn and silk mums, then set out baskets of individually wrapped supersize cookies, customers were wandering by in thick groups, undaunted by the gloomy weather and ready to enjoy a weekend of good food and innocent fun. By day's end, she'd almost forgotten the setting, the press of people, talk and laughter shifting the feel from academic to festive more than she would have thought possible, right up until a voice startled her from behind.

"I liked the vanilla caramels best."

A flicker of unease prickling her neck, Hannah choked down a sigh at the familiar boy's needy expression. "Dominic, right?"

He smiled, pleased she'd remembered, embarrassed almost, then gave a quick jerk of his head. "Yeah. Do you work at the cookie store, too?" His question referenced the banner displayed behind her, the words *Colonial Cookie Kitchen* flowing in old-world script.

Hannah nodded. "Sometimes. I work in the library in Jamison and the candy store, but when Meg has weekend festival booths, I try to help out. Would you like a cookie?"

He eyed them, hesitated, then flushed when she handed him two. "They're on the house."

"I've got money," he protested, but Hannah waved that off.

"Save it for something else or donate it to one of the good causes at the front. We have to start with fresh stock tomorrow so you're actually doing me a favor."

"Thanks." He took the cookies, his expression saying he wasn't sure how to handle her magnanimous action. In the end he headed down the hall, his shoulders a little straighter than they'd been. Several strides away, he swung back. "Thanks again, Miss—"

"Moore," Hannah told him. She widened her smile and shooed him away. "Go. Enjoy. And thanks for stopping by."

Her words surprised him, as if he couldn't fathom someone thanking him for just being there. Then he headed out the side door, one cookie rapidly disappearing.

Hannah noted his thinness and filed that alongside the personality quirks, the hand twitches and the uncertain eyes.

Was it something?

Nothing?

She had no clue, but instinct told her Dominic needed a friend.

"Time for supper." Jeff's voice broke up her thoughts, a

welcome diversion. "And don't tell me you snacked on cookies all day and don't want to eat because I'm starved."

"First, you're bossy," Hannah told him, sliding the meager remnants of the day's leftovers his way. "These are for you. Meg's dad already gathered my boxes and cash to take back to the store for tomorrow's load so we're good to go."

"As nice as this is," Jeff replied, hoisting the small box of cookies for her benefit, "it's not supper. And I don't know about you, but I didn't have a chance to eat all day."

"Me neither."

"Then I'm assuaging my guilt for not feeding you lunch by taking you out. I should have gotten over here midday but I got tied up at work. I know how crazy it is when you're running a booth on your own. It's hard to find a moment to get away."

"The hall runners offered to spell me so I could get food," Hannah admitted, but she wasn't about to explain why she refused, that the thought of walking the halls to get to the improvised food court made her go weak in the knees. "But I hate to eat on the run, so I figured I'd wait."

"All the more reason for me to feed you now," Jeff declared as he led the way out the front doors. The rain had let up slightly, but the late hour and thick clouds hung dark and foreboding. Jeff grasped her hand and headed for the shuttle bus at a run. "We'll grab our cars and head to the Texas Hot, okay?"

"Perfect."

"Callie said we signed up twenty-two significant sponsors today," he told her once they'd settled themselves into a booth at Wellsville's old-style restaurant. "That's a huge plus for little investment of time or effort."

"I'll say. And despite the bad weather, the fair did well. I was surrounded by happy vendors."

"I think the rain actually helped us," Jeff replied. "The

local corn mazes and hayrides got rained out. Since we had an indoor location, we got the spillover."

"And tomorrow…"

"Shorter hours, ten to three, then the Harvest Dinner."

She smiled, rimmed her water glass with a finger and sat back. "I'm glad I had time to help this year."

"Me, too." He glanced up as Ellie Ramos headed their way.

"You guys worked the festival and you're still hungry?" she asked, surprised. She handed them each a menu and shook her head. "Which means that business was so good there was no time to eat or they ran low on food around four o'clock."

"Right on both counts." Jeff grinned and didn't bother with the menu. "Ellie, nothing sounds better on a cold, wet day than your chicken and biscuits, smothered in gravy with a side of slaw."

"Make that two." Hannah handed her menu back to Ellie and added, "And if a chocolate cola happens to come my way, I wouldn't refuse it."

"Coffee for me."

"I'm on it."

Jeff studied Hannah once Ellie had gone, his gaze questioning.

"Why are you staring at me? Do I have something on my face?"

"No." He wavered, the tiny furrow between his eyes hinting concern, then said, "You looked a little shell-shocked at the school this morning and I was wondering if it was something I said. Or did."

Tell him.

A part of her wanted to, but not here. Not now. Revealing her part in the Ironwood massacre couldn't be relegated to casual dinner conversation. She met his look of concern and shrugged. "It pushed some old buttons."

"Do you want to tell me about them?"

"Another time?" She sat back as Ellie delivered their drinks, then glanced around the restaurant. "And in a more private setting."

"I'll hold you to that." His look of promise meant business. After talking with Jane the week before, Hannah realized that some people already knew her past and respected her privacy. She didn't want Jeff to hear about it from someone else, but Ironwood wasn't a subject she delved into lightly.

She took a sip of her blended soda and raised her glass in a toast. "To a successful day."

"Hear, hear." Jeff tapped her glass with his coffee mug. "I can't remember ever enjoying a Farmer's Fair so completely, Hannah."

Heat rose again. "You were barely there," she scolded lightly.

"In body, yes. But in thought?" He met her gaze with a sweet look of warm appreciation, his eyes saying more than mere words. "I was by your side all day."

His gentleness melted her, but did it make up for the dogged determination he gave to his job?

You equate too much with Brian, with the past. A good work ethic is something to thank God for.

"Food." He tapped her hand as Ellie approached. "And stop looking so serious. It's bad for your digestion."

She smiled in gratitude. "We'll talk sometime soon, okay?"

"It's fine, Hannah." His tone bathed her in reassurance, as if nothing she said or did could possibly make a difference. Hannah knew better, but was willing to take the chance because keeping her secrets was no longer possible. And maybe that was a good thing.

Chapter Thirteen

Jeff strode into the library for the scheduled Thursday night meeting, his expression grim. Protective instinct pushed Hannah forward, wanting to soothe his angst.

He spotted her and smiled, a heartfelt smile that softened the hard lines of his face for just a moment. He took his place at the end of the table, settled his notes, then addressed the group. "I apologize for being late. I was on the phone with my grandmother. She called me a few minutes ago to tell me Jane Dinsmore is gravely ill."

All eyes moved to the empty chair next to Hannah.

"She's in the hospital right now. According to my grandmother, she's been quietly fighting cancer for over three years. She'd been doing better until this summer, when a recurrence showed the cancer had metastasized to other parts of her body."

His expression reflected the pain of his words. "Most of us have known Miss Dinsmore since childhood, and we all understand what a loss her death would be to our community."

Reverend Hannity stood, apparently unsurprised by this news. He reached for the hands of those seated alongside him, then waited as the rest of the group followed suit. Silent for a moment, he lowered his chin and closed his eyes. "Father, we beseech Thee on behalf of our dear sister Jane, to love her, watch over her, care for her and guide her. We ask Your healing hands upon her if that is Your will, but more than that, Lord, we thank You for Jane Dinsmore, for her selfless life, her unselfish acts, her kindly, straightforward ways and her tireless commitment to the youth of our community. You blessed us with her love of science and teaching, and while our hearts grieve her illness, our souls appreciate what she has sacrificed for our children. Amen."

Hannah stared at the empty chair, little things suddenly making sense. The cough. The pale look. The breathlessness.

For a brief moment, Hannah wondered if her presence in Jamison, Jane's illness and now Hannah's gradual healing was all part of God's greater plan?

Of course not.

And yet...

She shut those thoughts down and concentrated on what Jeff was saying as he outlined the town board's approval of their stone walking path proposal, but the pall of Jane's illness took the shine off the excitement. By meeting's end, everyone was ready to go home, digest the news and think. Pray.

And that included Hannah. She stepped up to Jeff once the others had left and quietly put her arms around him from behind, hoping her presence offered comfort.

He didn't turn. He covered her hands with his and she felt the tremor within, the emotion he'd tamped down while conducting the meeting. She moved around front, laid her head against his chest and felt those strong arms engulf her. This time she was pretty sure she was holding him up, not vice versa. "I'm sorry, Jeff."

He tightened his grip. "Me, too. Jane's been Grandma's friend forever. They're peas in a pod, two of the most industrious women I've ever met. Grandma's not handling this well and Grandma handles everything well, so that's a real wake-up call."

Having met both women, Hannah saw the parallel. "Death's a tough thing to face. We can rationalize it through our faith but it's hard to minimize the physical loss of someone we love."

"Exactly." He held her close; the steady beat of his heart beneath her ear was a source of comfort and strength. When he pulled away, she saw the reluctance in his face, his eyes, and smiled.

"Thank you."

She moved back to the table, grabbed her jacket and shrugged into it while he gathered his notes in an uncharacteristic slapdash fashion.

He walked her to her car, pensive, and Hannah wished there was some way to help him through this. She might be a relative newcomer, but she'd sensed the feelings of the volunteers gathered tonight, and their heartfelt reaction said so much about Jane's effect. Hannah knew firsthand the positive ramifications of a good teacher. She rolled down the window to bid Jeff good-night, and his sad look made her wish she could help make this better.

"I'll talk to you tomorrow."

Hannah nodded, unable to smile, wishing things were all right. "Okay."

Jeff stepped back, watching as she drove away, but not really seeing her, Hannah was sure of it. As she climbed the steps to her apartment, she heard the sound of an engine. She turned, noting Jeff's car, and that made her smile.

He'd taken the time to make sure she'd gotten home okay. She raised her hand in acknowledgment, unable to see his answering wave, but for tonight, just the knowledge that he'd followed her home was enough.

***

Do it, her inner voice scolded the next evening.

Don't you dare, argued its alter ego.

She'd been living a tug-of-war since the previous night. She'd contemplated, stewed and prayed, unable to decide. Should she offer to take over Jane's classes, be the helping hand the school desperately needed? She was professionally self-confident enough to know that no one could do it better, but the question boiled down to could she do it at all?

She dropped her head into her hands, pensive, the late-day shadows marking the library's closing time. She'd locked the door but hadn't gone home yet, determined to sort this out. If only she could talk to someone.

Jeff.

Her heart agreed, but her head scolded. *He's going to find out eventually, why not just tell him? See what he thinks? He's the kind of guy that views the whole picture. He'll give you a fresh vantage point.*

And then maybe walk away forever, like Brian.

That thought crushed her fervor, but she couldn't let it die, so in the end she hit her speed dial and prayed. He answered right away. "Hey, I was just thinking about you. What's up?"

His gentle warmth, his choice of words, the way he looked at her when they were together… Could she risk losing that by revealing her past? Would the truth set her free or send him running? Either way, she needed to know, so she took a deep breath. "Can I talk to you?"

"Of course. Now?"

He didn't tease or joke around, unusual for him, but maybe he read the need in her voice. "Yes. Are you home? Can I come over?"

"I'm actually just pulling into the library parking lot because I knew you'd be closing up."

His thoughtfulness tightened her throat, making this confession that much harder. She had so much to lose, but she knew they didn't dare take this relationship further with Jeff in the dark. And right now she needed a friend, a confidant. Who better than the man she loved?

Loved? Admitting that sent anticipation shivering up her spine and fear roiling into her gut. "I'll be right out."

"I'll be waiting."

He met her by the steps, smiled and hauled her in for a bracing hug, his strong arms and broad chest warming her. "Rough day?"

"No. But I need to talk to you."

"Your place is close. Shall we head there?"

"Sure."

She climbed in her car and headed home, half wishing the drive was longer. Her festive porch lightened her mood as she climbed the steps. No matter what happened after today, she'd shared a wonderful time with Jeff, a delightful reprieve. And if that was all he was able to give after hearing her story, she'd be grateful.

You'll be brokenhearted, warned her conscience, more than a little self-righteous.

Yeah, but honest, shot back her good-girl ego. *The truth shall set you free, Hannah.*

He followed her in, set a bag in the kitchen, then grabbed her hand and led her to the couch in the front room. "Sit."

She followed his direction, not like there was much choice. He sat alongside her, leaned back and tugged her with him. "Okay. What's up?"

She couldn't do this sitting back, unable to see his face or read his reactions. She pushed forward and turned to face him. His left brow arched, wondering. She clenched and unclenched her hands, then dove in. "I told you I was a teacher."

He nodded. "Yes."

"I taught high school science for eight years."

"Impressive. Not an easy task."

"It was very easy," she corrected, working to keep her voice level. "I loved it. I loved it so much." Her voice cracked with that admission, just a little, but he noticed it. She could tell from the way his brow furrowed, the way he hunched forward slightly.

"Why did you stop, Hannah?"

Five little words that either led her forward or offered her an escape. She chose to move forward, fully aware of the risks. "I taught at Ironwood High."

He reached for her hand, his strong, sure fingers giving her strength, but the gravity in his eyes said he remembered Ironwood High, along with the rest of a grieving nation.

"We had developed a special class in conjunction with a program at Penn. It was an elective for students who met certain criteria, but I had the power to approve who should be in the class. The mission of the class required outside fieldwork and we developed a thoughtful selection process to give us a variety of kids. We were excited about this concept, because the class selection was actually part of the team research, the effect of nature and nurture on the human brain."

"To do this with high school kids half fascinates me and half scares me to death," Jeff told her, his gentle tone saying she could continue. "So you chose the class…"

"We had a committee," she explained, "but I had veto power because I was the teacher who would be out and about with this group. The administration let me weed out kids whose application might look okay, but whose personality might be detrimental in less structured settings. We had tons of applications but we limited the class to twenty, a nice number to work with."

"If you say so." His face said there was little fun involved with teaching twenty kids anything, but he squeezed her hand. "And then…"

She hauled in a breath and let it out on a sigh. "Brad Duquette was the mastermind behind the Ironwood massacre. Steve Shelwyn and Dave Mastrodonato were his disciples, but they didn't have the vision to put it together. Brad did. He was such a smart kid, but there was something about him. Something not right, as if he wanted help, but laughed at anyone's efforts because he knew he could outsmart them."

She shook her head, thinking back and still coming up short. "I saw that in him, and that's the reason I vetoed his application, because it always felt like he was trying to trip me up and I couldn't take that chance if I was out on my own with the kids, you know?" She met Jeff's gaze.

He nodded in support, and Hannah gripped his hands tighter. "What if I'd accepted him? Would it have been the tipping point, the one thing that gave him hope, that lessened his anger?"

"You can't take that on yourself, Hannah." Jeff closed the narrow space between them and pulled her in for a hug. "Out of all those applications, you could only accept twenty. The odds were against *all* of the applicants, but none of the others went on a shooting spree, right?"

"I know that." She pulled back and held his look, wishing she didn't have to burden him, but having little choice now. "But this one did. And when they entered the school during lunchtime, my research class was split, half in the lab, half in the adjoining classroom with me. We heard loud voices, then screaming, then gunfire. Karen Krenzer, the lab instructor, liked to keep our linking door closed during labs so my voice wouldn't distract her group. I'd left my keys on top of my desk because I was running late that morning, so I grabbed them and locked the adjoining door to the lab. A couple of boys barricaded it with a filing cabinet and a bungee cord while I locked the hall door.

"Between the bombs they rigged, the guns they used and

the sheer surprise of the attack, they managed to kill three teachers, nine students and two police officers who tripped a bomb as everything was happening. Fourteen people died that day because I denied Brad Duquette's application into my research class."

Chapter Fourteen

Her face had grayed. The pain of retelling the story was an obvious drain.

What a thing for her to carry around, this kid's lack of conscience, his deep-seated anger. None of that was Hannah's fault. "You can't shoulder that, Han. It's not fair. Whatever messed those kids up happened long before you came on the scene."

A tiny smile softened her face. "That's what Jane Dinsmore told me. She's known all along who I am, where I came from. So did your grandmother."

It didn't surprise Jeff that Grandma knew. She was thorough with everything she did and she chaired the council that hired Hannah, but the fact that she didn't say anything...

That felt a little off.

"They also knew Jane was sick, that she might not beat this cancer and if she didn't, I would be here, waiting in the wings."

The idea that Jane and his grandmother plotted to keep Hannah here because they wanted a teacher to step into Jane's shoes if she didn't win the battle with cancer... Of all the pompous, power-wielding—

"It was a brilliant idea, actually."

Hannah's words stopped his inner tirade. "What do you mean?"

She lifted her slim shoulders in a slight shrug. "They gave me a chance to heal, to reconnect with people, with God. With life. And you."

"Hannah, I—"

"I need to finish before you say anything else, Jeff. Please?"

Her soft and earnest plea made him relax his hands, his emotions. "Of course."

"Ten of my students were with me. Nine were in the lab with Karen, the lab instructor. One was absent. Once we barricaded the lab door and locked the hall door, we hid behind a half wall of shelving that was built like a study nook along the last three windows. We huddled there, crouched behind the shelving, listening to what happened in the lab, step-by-step."

Jeff didn't need to hear the details of that carnage. He remembered the ceaseless minute-by-minute news coverage and read the reality in her gray pallor, her heavy eyes.

"And while Brad tormented and shot Karen and those lab students, he shouted we'd be next, that I'd never get the chance to keep a kid out of a class again."

"Oh, Hannah." Jeff pulled her into his chest, needing to hold her, not sure what to say when words weren't enough. "Hannah. I'm so sorry."

"He couldn't get through the lab door. He sent Dave to the hallway to see if they could infiltrate our room through the hall entry doors, but the hall security gates came down when the emergency was sounded, and our security chief was a former county sheriff licensed to carry. He shot Dave as he approached our classroom door with a sawed-off shotgun and two homemade bombs. Ironwood is a huge school, and I found out later the reason Dennis found the shooters so quickly was because he followed the trail of bodies up the back stairs."

Jeff hung on, praying, begging God to bless her, help her, help those families whose lives were altered in the space of a few hours.

"When Brad realized he couldn't get through the lab doors, he started shouting the names of the captive students before he shot them. He made sure we heard them cry and plead. Beg for their lives. He had Steven list the names on the blackboard with the time of death, taunting the police for their lack of speed."

The magnitude of the combined depravity gripped Jeff, making him wish he could do something, anything to make this better. But no one could.

Except God.

"When Brad realized he'd lost Dave, he and Steve started raining bullets on our room through the wall. They managed to hit the windows above us." He didn't think she could pale further but he was wrong. Her eyes went wide, the sights and sounds of that horrific afternoon painting a mental picture he could only imagine. Hannah had no choice but to replay the events. She'd lived them. "We clung to one another, crouching low in a bed of sharp, broken glass while the rain poured in, lashed by forty-miles-per-hour winds."

"Lord, bless Hannah, help her to stay strong, to see Your words, Your truth in the goodness that lives in her. The strength, the wisdom, the amazing intelligence You've given her and the gift of giving she shares with others every day. Help her, Lord, take away the guilt she carries wrongly, help her see that evil cannot always be explained and that the devil's work should be condemned, not that of the innocent."

"Was I innocent, Jeff?" She pushed back and searched his gaze. "What if I let him into our room? Would he have still shot Karen and those students? Would it have bought time so that help could arrive?"

"You did the right thing, the brave thing," he insisted, amazed she'd think differently. "You saved lives that day, the lives of the kids in your classroom. You didn't cause the other deaths, Hannah. The shooters did. Don't take that on yourself. You reacted to a horrible situation with guts and brains. How can you think less of yourself?"

"Because he called me a coward for hiding."

The calm way she said the words chilled Jeff. He gripped her shoulders and held her gaze, hoping, praying he was doing the right thing. "You are one of the bravest people I've ever met, Hannah. You reacted to an out-of-control situation with thought and action. You saved ten children and yourself." When she looked like she might argue, he shook his head, needing her to understand. "I will forever thank God that you had the common sense to lock and barricade that door, that the barricade held and that the bullets he sprayed through the wall didn't hit anyone in your room."

He gathered her back in his arms, feeling her tears wet his shirt, his neck. He didn't know how long he cradled her like that, but when she finally sat up, he read the look of determination on her face and knew she'd made a decision.

"You're going for it, aren't you?" He leaned back, assessing her gaze, the set of her shoulders.

"I have to."

"Why?" Why would she put herself through that?

"Because I won't feel whole again until I face this fear, Jeff. It eats at me. I hide it away and think I'm better, and then it rises up at the worst times, choking me."

"Wouldn't therapy be easier?"

She leaned forward and laid her soft hand atop his arm. "This *is* therapy. My last step. I've come so far, but I need to go the distance, Jeff. Face the dragon."

"I'll buy you a dragon of your own. We can build him a pen in our backyard."

A soft smile chased the shadows for a moment. "*Our* back-yard?"

"Hannah, I—"

She put her hand over his mouth and shook her head. "Don't. Please. You have to know the rest, Jeff, that I came totally unglued after the attack. I was hospitalized for a while, and then was treated by a psychiatrist and a therapist for months. I hated myself, I hated my life, I hated the shooters and I wanted to die."

He didn't think his heart could break any further, but it did, seeing the guilt in her face for her very normal reaction to murdering chaos. "Hannah, you crashed afterward. That's normal."

"Nothing I did could be construed as normal," she argued, remembering.

"It was," Jeff insisted. "You're a scientist. You understand the principles of action/reaction. Your emotional *reaction* matched their actions, step-by-step. They attacked your students, your room, your colleague, your job and then your faith. You crashed and burned, then regrouped by coming here. Working here." He hugged her again, feeling the softness of her hair slip beneath his cheek, his hands. "And I'm so glad you did."

"Me, too."

He smiled, feeling her relax in his arms. "So you're going to apply for Jane's job?"

"Yes."

He had no idea if this was a good move or a really stupid one, but he knew one thing: whatever Hannah decided, he'd support her from this day forward. "Okay, then. Where do we start?"

"We?"

He nodded firmly. "I'm a big believer in facing the past. Moving on. Whatever happens, just know I've got your back."

"Really?"

"Absolutely."

"Well, then. Let's start with this." Hannah stood and crossed the room, disappeared for a few seconds, then returned, carrying a box.

Jeff frowned, not understanding.

She held out the box and pointed to the script. "This is from Brian. He was my fiancé at the time of the attack. He's now the vice president of VanDerstraat Communications and a town board member in Big Springs. He didn't have much use for me while I was in the psych wing."

"Hannah."

She waved him off. "In retrospect, he did us both a favor. I wasn't good for anyone or anything at that point. It taught me that true love is required to stand up to the test, that those vows of sickness and health are not just pretty words. They're a solemn pledge."

"So what's in here?"

She made a face and shook her head. "I don't know. I was tempted to chuck it to the curb when it came, but I realized that was the chicken's way out."

"So you shoved it away…" he teased.

"I wasn't *that* brave," she shot back, a tiny smile curving her mouth. "And notice that I'm opening it with you here, ensuring proper backup."

"Let's do this."

"All right." She tugged the tape free from the sides, then pulled the strip across the box top, the distinct sound leading them to what? More sadness? More sorrow?

Jeff was pretty sure that was humanly impossible.

"Oh."

Jeff leaned forward, his vision obscured by the box flaps, but he needn't have bothered. Hannah withdrew a presidential award for excellence in teaching math and science, her expression soft, her fingers trailing the vellum surface.

"Pretty impressive."

Her bittersweet smile said yes and no.

"May I see?"

She handed it over and withdrew a second one from the box. "Sure. You look at that one and I'll look at this one."

"You won two?"

She nodded. "My Penn projects. I was nominated three times and received the award twice."

"Hannah, that's amazing."

She shrugged the praise away. "It was a wonderful honor for me and the kids. Ah…" She grimaced, pulling out a sheet of folded paper, then sent Jeff a rueful look. "Oh, good. A note."

Jeff leaned over her shoulder, and read out loud. "Hannah, hope all is well. The school asked if I could forward these to you with their apologies. It seems they were lost for a while and the new principal is sorry they weren't sent to you years ago. Best, Brian."

Funny. She'd been worried about what Brian's message might do to her, but sitting here, reading his short words, seeing his script, it meant nothing. Not a thing.

Of course, six feet of wonderful and supportive man sitting alongside her had something to do with that. She crumpled the note into a tight ball and lofted a three-pointer into the small garbage can just inside the kitchen door.

"Sweet shot."

She smiled and flicked a look Jeff's way. "Old news."

"Good."

She lifted the beautiful award, stood and placed it in a position of prominence alongside Nick's family picture. "I'll go see Jane tomorrow."

Jeff stood and crossed the room with the second award. He set it up alongside the family photo, flanking Nick's accomplishments with Hannah's. "And you know I'll help in any way I can, right?"

His promise was worth so much more than he knew. Jeff's

faith, his work ethic and his level of commitment were so different from Brian's. How could she have ever thought the two men similar?

"They're beautiful, Hannah." Jeff nodded to the awards, then drew her into his arms, cradling her against his chest, his heart. "And so are you." He dropped his mouth to her hair, her cheek, kissing her gently. "You'll let me know if there's anything you need?"

"Will do."

"Do you want me to go with you tomorrow?"

"Nope."

"All right, then." He paused before he opened the front door. "Call me. Let me know how things go, okay?"

"I will."

He hated to leave after hearing her story. He climbed into his car to return to Wellsville, then paused, chagrined.

Hannah had dealt with more death and destruction in a few short hours than most people face in a lifetime. She'd crashed and burned, then rebuilt her life step-by-step, while he stubbornly refused to move beyond high school anger at his father and half brother. That realization said he had some serious fence-mending of his own to do.

He turned the car around and headed north toward Nunda, unsure where he'd find Matt, but determined to fix things now.

Chapter Fifteen

"Jane?" Hannah tiptoed into Miss Dinsmore's hospital room the next morning. Jane looked relieved, as if she'd been hoping Hannah would come. But then, Hannah had already figured that out. Hannah swallowed a sigh, mustered a smile and stepped in.

"I'm glad you're here."

"Me, too." She sat in the chair by the bed and grasped Jane's hand; the dry skin was lax beneath her fingers. "I had to, but you know that, don't you?"

Jane nodded. She paused long seconds, eyeing the wall, then dragged her gaze back to Hannah's. "Helen and I prayed when we found out I was sick. We asked God to send someone special, someone who could appreciate our children and towns. It's hard to get good teachers in these outlying schools, even with a nice quality of life. We're so far off the beaten path that young people pass us by. And then your application came in for the library position."

Hannah nodded. "I thought God might have had a hand in it," she confessed, then gave Jane a wry smile. "Now I see that it was just two bossy women engineering things along."

Jane met her gaze with a smile of her own and shook her head as she gripped Hannah's hand. "Except we know He sent you on purpose. There is a time for every purpose under the heaven."

"But three years ago I was a basket case," Hannah said, not trying to soften the skepticism in her tone.

Jane acknowledged the time frame with a slight wince. "You needed healing time. And I had a fight on my hands. But it looks like we've reached the turning point. Will you be my long-term sub, Hannah? Please? I've got my science team preparing for the Christmas break state science games, and we're in the thick of the first semester and you know I don't take that lightly."

"We have that in common."

"So?" Jane studied her face, her expression hopeful but resigned to whatever Hannah might say. She'd obviously put thought and prayer into this petition.

So had Hannah. She leaned forward and grasped Jane's hand. "Yes."

Jane's features softened, a layer of worry removed. She squeezed Hannah's hand, her grip strengthened by hope. "Thank you."

Helen's voice interrupted the moment. "You asked her?"

"She did. I assured her you were both crazy. I'm a librarian now." Hannah gave Jane's hand a reassuring squeeze, letting her in on the joke.

"A librarian with a master's degree in biology and education," Helen retorted as she moved into the room. "Three Ironwood Central School Teacher of the Year awards and three nominations to the President's Award for Academic Excellence in Math and Science, two of which you won." She grasped Hannah's free hand and squeezed, imploring. "I wouldn't ask if the need weren't so great. Will you consider stepping in, taking over Jane's classes? Please?"

"Helen." Jane's deep tone drew Helen's attention.

"Yes?" Helen faced Jane, her concern evident. Jane nodded

toward Hannah and smiled. "She's already said yes. Stop annoying her."

"Really?"

"Really."

Hannah met Helen's gaze, amused. "Since seeing Helen beg is a rare occurrence, I'm noting the day and time in my PDA." She paused, all kidding aside, and swept both women a look. "The better question is, *can* I do this?"

"Yes."

"Of course you can." Helen's agreement sounded more vigorous than Jane's for various reasons. First, she'd never had to deal with a room full of hormone-stricken teenagers.

Helen thought everyone was invincible. Hannah had proven that wrong once, did she have what it took to try it again?

"God gifted you with a rare talent, Hannah Moore." Helen drew up a chair alongside Hannah and set her small purse down on the bed. "Don't allow evil to steal that gift or shroud that light under a bushel."

"What do we need to do?"

"The board needs a copy of your application, transcripts and the letters of recommendation you used when applying for the library job. Luckily I already have that."

Hannah wasn't surprised. This was Jeff's grandmother, after all.

"I've already downloaded your information into the database," Helen went on. "So all you need to do is fill out the forms attached to the email I'm about to send you and we'll proceed from there."

"You've begun the process already?"

Helen didn't even try to act embarrassed. "Weeks ago, when I saw you sparring with my grandson at our initial meeting."

"It's not hard to see where he gets his driven personality from," Hannah noted, her wry tone spurring Jane's smile.

A nurse stepped in, gestured to the clock and said, "Five minutes. She needs to rest."

"'Plenty of time for that in the grave,'" Jane barked. Hannah stood and laid a calming hand on her shoulder.

"Benjamin Franklin," she noted. She gave Jane's shoulder a gentle squeeze. "I love that quote. It's one of my favorites."

"Mine, too." Helen rose, walked around the foot of the bed and leaned down to hug her friend. "We'll go straighten out the details. You work on getting better."

"Helen."

"Don't throw in that towel without a fight, Jane."

Jane sighed. "I've been fighting, Helen. Maybe it's time…"

"See what they say in Buffalo, okay?" Helen turned toward Hannah again. "They're sending her up to Roswell for an evaluation. If they say there's no hope…" She shifted her gaze back to Jane. "Then we'll talk. But until then, we fight."

"We?"

Helen laughed, hugged her again and shrugged a shoulder toward Hannah. "I helped with this, didn't I?"

Jane yawned and smiled, fatigue weighting her eyes. "You did."

"Well, then."

Hannah studied Helen as Jane's eyes drifted closed. The stark worry was apparent, but when Helen pivoted, her features were calm, business as usual. "How soon do you think you can have that paperwork filled out?"

"This afternoon."

Helen's smile made Hannah feel ten feet tall, but the fear nagging her gut made her wonder what she was doing. She could have said no with no hard feelings on either side. She knew that.

But she *had* to say yes, uncertain if that was conscience or God-willed or a combination of the two. In any case, Hannah

Moore was about to retake her place at the front of a class-room, and hopefully wouldn't lose her breakfast doing it.

You'll be fine, you'll be fine, you'll be fine....

Whatever strings Helen pulled to put Hannah in front of the classroom Monday morning were quite impressive, but then this was Helen Walker they were talking about. Hannah approached the school bright and early. Her cell phone rang as she climbed the steps. She saw Jeff's number and answered quickly. "It wouldn't take much to talk me out of this right now, so if that's what you're hoping, now's your chance."

He laughed, which was the best reassurance she could ask for. "Not on your life, I called to encourage you and tell you I'm thinking of you. Got your lunch?"

"Right here."

"And your pencils are all sharpened?"

"Yes, Mom."

He laughed again. "I just wanted you to know I'm praying for you. Thinking of you. Caring about you."

Her heart swelled to impossible proportions. His tender words pushed her to succeed. "Thank you, Jeff. Oops, gotta go. Even teachers aren't supposed to use cell phones in the school."

"A rule that gets broken regularly, I expect. Have a good day, Hannah."

"I will. You, too."

She walked through the doors and nodded to the security guard seated to the left. Hannah wondered what it would have been like to teach a few decades ago, when the idea of school security was a vice principal. Now teams of former sheriffs and police patrolled district schools, and even with all that, assaults happened.

"Hannah?" A woman stepped forward, tall and solid, her short, crisp haircut framing a strong but kindly face. "I'm Laura Henning, the principal."

"Nice to meet you." Hannah accepted Laura's hand and hoped the older woman couldn't feel her thrumming pulse. She looked around. "It's a beautiful school."

"And a little scary right now, I'd expect."

"Downright terrorizing, but I made it this far." Hannah gave the entry a look as they moved to the stairs. "And not to belabor a bad thing, can you give me a mental sketch of security? It helps me preplan a course of action."

"Did you learn that in therapy?" Laura asked as they climbed the wide stairway.

"Nope. In fourth grade during fire safety week. I always scout out my options in the light of day so my brain can kick in as needed."

"That's remarkable."

Hannah sent her a small smile. "It gets the job done. And it helped at Ironwood, because I always have a plan of action in the back of my mind."

Laura nodded, turned left and headed down a hall. "I'll have one emailed to you as soon as I'm back in my office. You have a computer here on your table, a printer alongside, and you're one of only two computer stations with full access to the internet. Most stations have limited access, but Jane was given a reprieve because of the research nature of her methods."

"Wonderful."

She thought she'd hate stepping into the classroom, thought she'd go a little crazy inside, but she loved it. It felt like coming home. The science room was cluttered enough to be user-friendly, the walls covered with great quotes, equations and thoughtful insights Jane commandeered for motivation.

"Give me a call if you need anything." Laura passed along her direct access code to Hannah. "We have security checkpoints on each floor, but there's been little need for them. Still…"

Hannah nodded, understanding. "You never know."

"Exactly. Here is your schedule. I'm having Rose Tomer assist for the first few days. She knows the kids and might be able to defuse any situations that come along."

"A babysitter?" Hannah tipped her head slightly, one brow up, facing Laura directly.

"A facilitator," Laura replied, meeting Hannah's look with frank honesty. "One of these little darlings is going to look you up, see who you are and start asking questions."

Hannah's heart dropped to somewhere in the vicinity of her left foot.

"Rose's presence allows you the option to step away if necessary. And maybe I'm wrong, maybe it won't happen—"

Hannah waved her off as she settled things into her desk. "Oh, it will. I've been working with kids long enough to know that. Having Rose here gives me leverage. Thank you."

Her calm acceptance eased Laura's features. She nodded, then backed toward the door. "Remember, if you need anything…"

Hannah held up the slip of paper with her code. "I'm covered."

"All right."

Once Laura left, Hannah breathed a sigh. The rumble of buses drew her attention to the window, the winding Genesee River a beautiful sight as the sun's rays pinked the hilltops beyond.

Ready or not, here they come.

Jeff's car idled alongside hers when she came out of school at five-fifteen. He climbed out and came toward her, his expression wondering until she stepped beneath a parking lot light. He took one look at her face and relaxed into a smile. "It went well."

"Very well." Hannah hunted for words to express her feelings, then settled for a shrug. "I was fine."

"One of us isn't surprised." Jeff pulled her in for a hug. The feeling of being in his arms warmed her despite the cold, bleak afternoon. "Congratulations, Hannah."

She stepped back, trying to remain objective. "It was just one day. I taught long enough to know that's not necessarily indicative of success, but…" She smiled and slanted her gaze up to his. "It felt great."

"Good." He grasped her shoulders and jerked his chin toward their cars. "Can I buy you supper?"

"Don't I wish." She held up her bag as proof. "Lesson planning. I stayed late to get an idea of where Jane was going, but if I'm doing this, I'm doing it right. I'll be lesson planning for this week's classes tonight, then for the month over the weekend."

"But you need to eat."

She nodded. "I ordered a sub from the deli. Tomorrow night, tuna. Wednesday, who knows? But we could get together before the meeting on Thursday. How does that sound?"

He sent her an exaggerated frown. "Like life just got lonelier on me."

She grinned, poked his shoulder and headed for her car. "Presidential science awards come with a price tag, my friend."

"I see that. But you know what else I see?"

Hannah turned, Jeff's warm smile a blanket of comfort in the dull, gray cold. "What?"

"The woman you were born to be." He reached out, tucked a strand of her hair back behind her ear and let his hand linger along the side of her face, his tender smile approving. "And it's wonderful, Hannah."

Hannah glanced around, sighed and smiled, amazed and satisfied, unable to disagree. "It sure is."

"Knock it off, guys," Hannah scolded a group of girls in a first-floor hallway the next day. "Does what Chrissie said to Amelia really matter in the worldwide scheme of things to care about?"

Two of the girls flushed. A third rolled her eyes, her expression saying Hannah was out of touch. Hannah sent the fourth girl a knowing look. "And lose the cell phone. You know you're not supposed to have it out during the day."

"But…"

Hannah arched a brow, glanced at her wrist to show she hated wasting time and tapped her foot.

"Sorry, Miss Moore."

"Thank you, Angie. And for your information, ladies—" she leaned in, inviting their confidence "—I think Chrissie's wrong. Randy Lessman *is* that cute. Totally."

Angie blushed while the other girls laughed. Hannah was glad to see some things never changed. As she rounded the corner to the teacher's lounge, a young man stepped in front of her, angling left while she turned right. She stopped short of bumping into him, then smiled and put a hand on his arm. "Dominic, right?"

"Hey." He nodded, not smiling but looking pleased to meet her. "You work here now, too?"

"I'm Miss Dinsmore's long-term sub. Are you taking science this year?"

"AP Physics."

Hannah paused, surprised. "How old are you?"

"Sixteen."

"That's a hefty load. Do you like physics?"

"Hate it."

She gave him a sympathetic look. "Then why take it?"

He shrugged. "I'm smart. My dad is a physics professor at Alfred University."

"A chip off the old block, huh?"

The vehement shake of his head came quicker than Hannah would have liked. "No."

"Then just be yourself, Dominic," Hannah advised. "If

you're good at science, it's an easy A for you, but it's okay to follow your own path."

"You don't know my father."

"True enough. Hey, if you ever want to talk or go over science stuff, I'm here after school." Dominic's lost-puppy demeanor tugged at Hannah's heart. "And the science team is prepping for the Christmas contest. Have you ever thought of joining us?"

"No." He paused, a mix of regret and angst painting his features. "I don't have time for that stuff."

"Well, if you find time, come see me," Hannah told him, remembering the bereft look she'd seen at their first meeting in the candy store. "We're weak in physics and could use your help. Of course, understanding the physical properties driving molecular biology would be a huge help…."

His brightened expression said she'd dangled good bait. "I'm doing a paper on processes for interrupting or diverting proteins to block the spread of cancer."

"Wonderful." Hannah put a gentle hand on his arm. He didn't flinch, a good sign. "Come find me anytime. Maybe we can solve the world's problems together."

She laid the phrase lightly, telling the boy she'd help if she could, but not enough to make him feel targeted.

"Maybe."

"Good enough."

He headed down the hall, head bowed, his hands thrust deep in his pockets, the abject picture of a singular young man.

"Problems?"

Hannah turned and found Laura approaching her. "No. Just a conversation with a kid."

Laura followed the direction of Hannah's gaze, pursed her lips and sighed. "Rough situation. Mother died of a self-inflicted gunshot wound when he was seven. He's brilliant, introverted, hates his stepmother and has been in therapy for as long as I've known the family. They moved here when he was eleven, thought it might help him to be in a new place."

Hannah thought of the interaction she'd witnessed between the stepmother and the boy. A change of setting that didn't address the verbal abuse of a sensitive kid wouldn't accomplish much. "I invited him to sit in on the science team practices."

"So did Jane. He refused."

Hannah shrugged. "Well, the invitation's been issued again. We'll see."

"Everything's going okay?"

Laura's cautious note said she was willing to let Hannah find her way. The fact that she'd found it so easy delighted Hannah. "Wonderful, actually. The *thought* of coming back intimidated me far more than the reality. I'm having the time of my life."

"That's what Rose said." Laura met Hannah's look. "She told me you're a marvel and the kids are eating out of your hand."

Hannah laughed. "Her assessment's a mite generous, but we're having fun and they're learning. It's all good."

"Glad to hear it. And now I must go convince Mr. Bernard to stop haranguing the staff for overuse of paper towels in the ladies' rooms."

"Good luck with that."

Laura smiled. "Thanks. I'll need it. And Hannah?"

"Yes?"

"Good job."

Hannah smiled, the heartfelt praise a blessing. "Thank you."

Chapter Sixteen

Jeff did an internet search for Cavanaugh Construction Thursday morning. Several entries popped up, along with a few current images. Jeff couldn't miss Matt's tough gaze or firm expression, but they were balanced by fairness in his eyes, a welcome new addition. He punched Matt's number into his cell phone, determined. He'd scoured the Nunda area on Friday night, but came up with nothing. One way or another, he needed to see Matt. Talk with him face-to-face. Settle old wrongs.

Matt answered with no preamble. "What's up, Jeff?"

His quick tone tweaked Jeff, but that wasn't Matt's fault. "I need to see you."

"Why?"

"Nothing I can go into over the phone. Where are you?"

Matt didn't answer the question. Instead he said, "Your house. Fifteen minutes."

Jeff stood and headed for the door. "I'm on my way."

He pulled into his driveway and parked alongside Matt's black truck, wondering what to say. As he reached to open his car door, he glanced heavenward. "I could use guidance here. And maybe a clue about when to talk and when to shut up."

He climbed out of the car, motioned Matt to come in and opened the front door, the home's warmth a welcome reprieve from a sharp wind. Matt strode in behind him, eyed the door, then Jeff. "A heavier grade storm door will block that wind and keep the house warmer."

Jeff grimaced. "I actually know that. Just haven't gotten to it yet."

Matt angled him a look and folded his arms. "And you've lived here how long?"

"Eight years."

"Uh-huh." Matt's face said he wasn't surprised. "So. What's so urgent?"

Jeff waved toward the living room. "Come in. Sit down."

"Remembering our past discussions, I probably should stay close to the door," Matt argued, matter-of-fact. "That gives me easier access when you throw me out."

Jeff deserved that. And more. He jerked a thumb toward the comfortable living room. "Come in, sit down and let me get through this, okay?"

Matt studied Jeff's face before obliging him. "All right." He settled into a chair and clasped his hands. "Go for it."

Jeff sat opposite him, praying the right words would come now that he'd forced the issue. "We need to find some kind of common ground if we're both going to live down here."

Matt shrugged. "If by 'we,' you mean 'you,' I couldn't agree more. One of us refuses to fight."

Jeff grimaced, sheepish. "And that just ticked me off even more."

"Listen." Matt hunched forward, his face grim but honest. "I get that you have reason to hate me, that I symbolize all that was bad about our father, but part of making my own way was for me to come back down here. Fix what I can. Make things better."

"Penance?"

"Atonement. I messed up big-time when I was a kid. I've

got a lot to make up for, and it would be easier if you didn't try to get in the way."

"The town council."

"Exactly." Matt met his look dead-on. "You almost brought the whole deal down by speaking to them behind the scenes. My lawyer stepped in and cleared things up, but that was a cool three hundred extra I shouldn't have had to pay."

"You're right." Jeff shook his head, chagrined. "I was being a jerk."

Matt didn't disagree.

"But a smart person told me I needed to get over myself and change my attitude."

"Your mother."

Jeff eyed him, surprised. "How would you know that?"

"Because there were only two people who bothered to visit me while I was in juvie. My grandfather. And your mother."

Jeff stared, stunned. "No one else?"

"No."

"Your mother?"

"Busy running with man after man once news of her affair with Neal Brennan came out. She pretty much forgot she had a son. She died during my first tour in Iraq."

"And your father? Don Cavanaugh?"

"Decided that because he wasn't really my father biologically, there was no need to be one physically. He hit the bottle and hasn't stopped yet."

Jeff processed this news, then wondered how Matt could have turned out as normal as he now appeared. Matt answered the question for him.

"Your mother came to see me once a week. She brought me books and cookies. She constantly reminded me that kids make mistakes, but nothing is unfixable. She gave a mother's love to a kid who made her and her family the target of back-door gossip and never once made me feel guilty or undeserving."

"I guess that was my job." Jeff frowned and scrubbed a hand across the nape of his neck. "And your grandfather?"

"A great man who loved building things. Gentle. Kind. He took me in and helped me see where I went wrong and how to do things right. He died during my second tour."

"So you've got—"

"It's me and God." Matt stood, rolled his shoulders and glanced at his watch. "But I've got things that have to be done so I can close this deal as soon as the bank calls. We're already three weeks behind, and that's a killer for construction this time of year."

Jeff stood and extended his hand. "I want you to accept my apology for being a jerk, for forgetting that you're my brother."

Matt didn't reach out. "Accidental biology. We can leave it at that, Jeff."

"We can't." Jeff stepped forward, determined. "I was wrong. And stupid. First because I was a kid, then because I wasn't smart enough to see things the way they were. You'll get no more trouble from me, Matt. Ever."

"Listen, Jeff, this is nice but unnecessary." Matt met his gaze and Jeff read the strength there. The sincerity. How had he missed that before? "I'm down here just long enough to finish up Cobbled Creek, make amends, then go on my merry way. I'm not here to stay or infringe on your life."

"Then I'll hope you change your mind." Jeff kept his hand out, refusing to cave. "Because you've got family here and family takes care of one another. I'm just sorry I didn't realize that sooner."

His words touched Matt. He saw it in the softer expression, and when Matt's hand clasped his in a firm handshake, Jeff knew he'd done the right thing, finally. "We'll see."

Jeff nodded and followed Matt out the door. "That's good enough for now," he continued as Matt headed for the truck.

"But when you get invited to Thanksgiving dinner at Mom's, just remember, I call dibs on a drumstick."

Matt's slight smile held traces of doubt Jeff hoped to wipe away with time. "Luckily there are two. See ya."

He swung open the cab door, but Jeff caught the edge before he could swing it shut. He thrust his chin toward a bundle stowed behind Matt's seat. "Are you sleeping in this truck?"

Matt's chagrin was answer enough.

"Bunk here," Jeff urged him, waving to the house. "There's plenty of room."

Matt leveled him a look of disbelief. "I don't think we're at the sleepover stage yet." He jerked his chin toward the sleeping bag and pillow. "I gave up my apartment in Nunda because I expected the closing to be done sooner and that forty-minute drive would eat up too much of my workday. Nipping first and last month's rent plus a security deposit out of my bank account right now could ruin the deal, so I'm laying low. Once papers are signed, I'll find a place."

"I'm barely here," Jeff told him, then realized how sad that assertion was. "If you change your mind, the offer's open."

"I appreciate it." Matt gave him a quick nod and swung the door shut.

Jeff watched him go, wishing he'd had the wisdom to do this long ago. As Matt pulled away with a quick wave, Jeff realized something else.

His mother might not have the fast-forward attitude of his grandmother, but she'd showed a strength and wisdom he hadn't fully appreciated. Despite the embarrassment she suffered because of his father, she visited Matt. Ministered to him. Made him feel special and beloved, while Jeff spent two decades harboring grudges.

That realization made him more eager to change things up. With God's help and a humble spirit, he might be able to do just that.

* * *

"Hannah Moore. You still live around here?" Jeff joked when he arrived for their weekly fundraising meeting that evening.

She looked up from sorting papers and laughed. "I do. But thanks to you and your grandmother, I'm pretty much living in the classroom. Luckily Melissa is doing a wonderful job here." She swept the substitute librarian a fond glance.

"And it's going fine?" Jeff studied her face, looking for evidence otherwise.

She nodded. "Wonderful. Almost as if I never left."

"Good."

She handed him a stack of folders. "If you could set these around the table, I'll turn on the coffeemaker."

"Will do."

Callie Burdick walked in as Jeff set up the table. She moved his way, her expression expectant. "I heard you went to bat for us with the town council, Jeff. Thank you."

Jeff took a moment before looking up, choosing his words carefully, wishing he'd never asked the council members to block Matt's building permits, especially with Matt's involvement. "It was worth a try, Callie. But with the property in the bank's hands, there's not much anyone can do."

"I know," she told him, earnest. "But you tried and I have faith that everything will turn out all right."

It couldn't. Not for both parties, anyway, and Jeff knew that. He fumbled for words, then saw Hannah watching them, an eyebrow arched as she read his discomfort. She approached them, gave Callie a quick hug and nodded toward the coffee center. "The regular is brewed and decaf's on its way."

"You read my mind."

Callie headed for the coffee while Hannah turned toward Jeff. "You're playing her."

Jeff shook his head, adamant. "I'm not."

"You know more than you're saying."

He couldn't deny that. Not to Hannah. "Yes."

"Then that's playing her and I thought we had this discussion a long time ago."

"This is different, Hannah."

She sent him a look of quiet disappointment, her gaze shadowed in reality. "It always is, Jeff."

The arrival of other committee members thwarted further conversation, and when Hannah left Melissa to lock up without saying goodbye, Jeff knew they'd backpedaled. But he'd promised Matt confidentiality and no further interference. He couldn't go back on his word. And he'd told Callie the truth. If the bank approved Matt's application to mortgage the Cobbled Creek subdivision, no one could stand in his way. Nor should they.

But Matt's gain would be Callie's father's loss and Jeff felt the sting of that, wishing he'd never interfered.

A part of Hannah said she shouldn't get hung up on Jeff's actions.

Another part laughed out loud.

Hadn't she traveled this path before? Painted air castles with a man who put the bottom line first and foremost? Hadn't she learned her lesson then?

Obviously not.

She headed into school the next morning, determined to focus on one thing: reestablishing her teaching career. Laura's voice hailed her as she made her way down the entry hall, mentally preparing herself for a day of parent-teacher conferences.

"Hannah, I'm glad I caught you."

Hannah turned. "What's up?"

"I need you to sit in on a couple of conferences today."

"For?"

"Content appraisal," Laura explained. "One of the AP

teachers has come down with the flu, and the other one went out on emergency maternity leave yesterday. I need a content teacher on board for two conferences because they were parent requested."

"What time?"

"Two-fifteen and six-thirty."

Hannah frowned. "The two-fifteen is fine, but I've got a full schedule until six forty-five. Can you reschedule the later one for seven?"

"I'll make it work," Laura assured her. "And I'll send you the info you need on both. And since these are both strong students, there's no major stuff involved, although Mr. Fantigrossi can be tedious. Hopefully we can close them out in the allotted fifteen minutes with no problem."

"Wonderful, because I'm not nearly as diplomatic at 7:00 p.m. as I am at 7:00 a.m."

Laura flashed her a smile as she veered toward the office. "I couldn't agree more."

Dominic was actually Dominic Fantigrossi III.

Mental red flags sprang up the minute his father stalked into Hannah's classroom that evening. She read Laura's look of caution and stepped forward, her hand extended as a young math teacher trailed behind, looking intimidated. "Mr. Fantigrossi, I'm Hannah Moore. Pleased to meet you."

"I'd say the same, except I'm wondering why I'm here at all. In the first place—" one imperative finger was quickly joined by others as he listed his complaints "—my appointment was rearranged with little concern for my schedule. I'm conferencing with a teacher who has no bearing on my son's progress, therefore limiting the efficacy of this conference. And thirdly, I've been kept waiting ten minutes beyond our scheduled time. Already I'm not happy and this meeting hasn't even begun."

"Is Dominic coming?"

"I'm here."

Young Dominic shrugged into the room with reluctance, as if each step grew more difficult. He flicked a possible glance of apology to Hannah, but it was gone too quick to be sure.

"You're late." Dominic Senior's voice cut the kid no slack. Dominic squirmed, obviously uncomfortable. "I'm sorry."

"I would hope so." His father squared his shoulders, imposing. "Seven o'clock means seven o'clock." He shifted his glare to Laura. "In the real world, that is."

Hannah bit back words of retort, refusing to spar with him. Her last two meetings ran late, but those things happened on a long conference day. She'd learned to accept the missed or late appointments. Obviously, the elder Dominic didn't embrace a similar attitude.

She let Laura steer the meeting and kept her face placid. She'd gone over the boy's grades and the teacher's report, noting the only negative was lack of participation. Dominic's aptitude ranked high and his retention put him at genius levels, all things a parent should embrace with joy.

Not in this case.

While Hannah presented Dominic's science records to his father, she flashed encouraging smiles in the boy's direction, wanting him to jump in. Take part.

He didn't. Chin down, he gazed at his feet, right up until Hannah mentioned the science team. "I've asked him to join because we could use his help, but he's managed to put me off so far." She sent Dominic a friendly grin, trying to draw him in, right before his father's reaction demonstrated her faux pas.

"He refused?"

Too late, Hannah realized her mistake. The senior Dominic wasn't the kind of father that allowed his son to find his own way. Hadn't the boy's words hinted that? And now she'd gone and opened up Pandora's box for the kid, which was the last thing she wanted to do.

"Dominic knows the option is there," Hannah replied smoothly, trying to gloss over the father's reaction. "In the meantime, we can concentrate on his excellent grades, his potential and his work ethic, all of which highlight what a great kid he is."

"And that's fine if you're raising an average kid," countered the senior Fantigrossi. "I'm not. My son has more potential in his little finger than most kids dream of, so don't talk down to me with your edu-speak gibberish about looking at the bright side. Dominic understands that good grades aren't enough to get into the top schools, that he needs to be well-rounded, and since he bombed at sports—" the boy winced, the father's careless words cutting deep "—and he's not gifted musically, utilizing greater potential by joining the science team would help round out his profile. Why didn't you run this by me?" he demanded, confronting his son.

The boy shrugged. "I didn't think it was important."

Dominic's faint words made Hannah's heart cringe. His body language echoed his speech, a slight inward curl hunched his shoulders, his back, his arms, as if ducking blows, but the shots he took were aimed at his mental and emotional well-being, obviously a popular target.

"If it's any help, my invitation stands," Hannah announced.

"I'll think about it." The kid didn't look at her, but his voice said joining the science team ranked last on his list, especially now.

"You'll do it."

"I—"

"Mr. Fantigrossi…"

Dominic's father raised an imperious hand, concluding the meeting and silencing the staff. "This is not open for discussion. You have the room on the team." He pointed toward Hannah, then toward Dominic. "And you have plenty of time. End of story, and this meeting. Let's go."

Dominic stood. Hannah read the anger in his face, in his

eyes. She mouthed a quiet apology, but the boy maintained a cool gaze, his demeanor saying what he couldn't verbalize.

What started out as an easy day for her had ended poorly. Hannah longed to call Jeff and seek his opinion, but after last night's interchange with Callie, she realized her romantic instincts might still be unreliable, and that knowledge bit deep.

By the time she crawled into bed, the room bore the distinct odor of dead mouse, the newest victim of the landlord's attic poison, which meant it would only smell worse by morning.

Great.

Chapter Seventeen

Hannah answered the candy store phone the next afternoon. The busy Saturday marked the typical fall upswing in sales. With holidays approaching, people were stocking up or placing orders, keeping them hopping.

"Grandma Mary's Candies, this is Hannah, how can I help you?"

"Why did you tell him about the science team?"

Hannah's heart stopped, the cold, despairing voice setting off her internal warning system. "Dominic?"

"I told you no, didn't I?"

"Yes, but…" With customers moving around the store, Hannah couldn't think straight to direct this conversation. "Dominic, I…"

"No one listens to me," the boy explained, his tone aggrieved but not angry, which only made matters worse. Honest anger provided a release. Bottled misery could ignite in more dangerous ways.

"I'm listening, Dominic."

"No, you're not. You're wondering how to get me off the phone so you can take care of all those customers."

He was watching her.

A chill climbed Hannah's spine. Goose bumps dotted her

arms, but she grabbed hold of herself emotionally and kept her voice firm. "If you're close enough to see me—" she raised her gaze and did a visual scan of the street, but didn't catch sight of the boy "—then come over, munch on some caramels and talk to me. I didn't mean to mess things up. I'm new to the school, so your situation with your father took me by surprise. I'm sorry, kiddo, I realized my mistake too late and now you're stuck with me."

"I'm not."

I'm not? Hannah tried to gauge the boy's cryptic response. Was he expressing simple anger? Desperation? Suicidal options? Homicidal tendencies? Teens were notorious for reacting to things too quickly, kind of like that group of girls earlier that week.

Only the girls seemed normal, if a little overzealous.

Dominic didn't.

She waved to Megan as her friend finished boxing a large assortment, grabbed a notepad and headed into the kitchen area, pretending she was taking an order. "I'm in the kitchen now, you've got my full attention, so talk. And let me just say, having an overbearing father is tough, but you've got lots of people who care about you, starting with me. So promise me right now you're not going to do something foolish, something we'll both regret."

"Are you going to call the police? Tell them I called you?"

Hannah weighed her words carefully. "If I think you're a threat to yourself or others, then yes. If you're using me as a sounding board, then no. You got caught in a situation I was partially responsible for and I'm sorry, but other than apologizing and making your science team experience fun, I've got nothing. But if giving the science team a try means calming things with your father, why not just do it?"

"It's not that easy."

"Oh, it is," Hannah assured him. "You're making it difficult because you're mad. And caramels are a great stress reliever. All that chewing does wonders for the soul."

"Are you tempting me in so you can call the cops and have me put in the hospital against my will?"

Hannah tried to balance the situation with pre-Ironwood common sense in a post-Ironwood mind, and that was tough, but at least this kid was reaching out.

Father, help him. Comfort him. Sustain him with Your gentle hands, Your loving arms.

"And mess with all that drama? Please, it's Saturday, I turn on my no-drama-zone force field the minute I walk out of the school. Come in here, talk face-to-face and eat candy."

"Really?"

"Yes. Consider it candy store therapy. It works wonders for me."

She walked back out front as he came through the door, his bearing less timid than last night. "Dude."

The one-word greeting made him smile. "Miss Moore."

She held out a small tray of candies and plastic gloves. "Wash your hands, put these on and keep people happy for a few minutes, okay? We're swamped."

He paused, startled, then made a face. "You want me to help you?"

Hannah pointed toward the front. "See all those people? If we feed them, they might not stampede the counter."

A small smile softened his jaw as he surveyed the room. He nodded, washed his hands and donned the gloves. "Will you get in trouble for doing this?"

"Commandeering free help? That's every businessman's dream. Now get going. Time's wasting."

He moved forward, carrying the tray more like a shield, but by the time he'd made a pass through the crowd, he'd relaxed and actually exchanged smiles with a few customers.

And those smiles told Hannah that Dominic Fantigrossi III might be all right with a little tender loving care.

"We need more," he announced a few minutes later as Hannah cashed out a customer.

"The sample trays are in the kitchen. They're marked, and make sure you avoid anything with nuts, okay?"

"Anaphylactic shock being a bad advertising ploy."

Hannah grinned at his joke. "Exactly. Now you're catching on."

And he was. He hung out for the afternoon, handing out samples and bagging orders. He even emptied the garbage cans at closing time. By the time they locked up at eight o'clock, he looked tired but pleased, exactly what Hannah had hoped for.

But was it enough or too little, too late?

She had no idea.

Hannah's cell phone rang just after she arrived home. The Illinois area code listed no name. Hannah hesitated, then grasped the phone, trepidation snaking up her spine. "Hello?"

"Hannah Moore?"

"Yes."

"This is Jill Kantry, Christi Kantry's mother."

Hannah's heart fluttered. Christi had been one of the last students killed in Karen's lab class. "You got my note, Mrs. Kantry?"

"We did." A short pause followed before Jill continued. "I've put you on speaker. Is that okay?"

"Of course. And I just want to say I'm sorry I didn't send that note sooner. I—"

"Miss Moore, this is Jacob Westman."

"And Thomas Kwitchik."

"And Anna Li Phan."

"And…"

Hannah interrupted the litany of voices. "You're all there?"

Jill's voice came through again. "The ones still in this area. If it was possible, we'd have all hopped on a plane to come see you, but this seemed more expedient and afford-able. Miss Moore, our consensus is that while your notes of apology were well received, they were unnecessary."

"Totally unnecessary," someone else added.

"But…"

"You offered our children amazing opportunities at Iron-wood," Jill interrupted her. "We realize that and felt honored to have our kids work with you. We just want you to know that the unrighteous acts of others can never negate the dedi-cation and devotion our children received from you and Ms. Krenzer. And that's all we wanted to say."

Hannah stopped, searching for words and coming up short. "You're thanking me?"

"And wishing you well," added a strong male voice. "God bless you, Miss Moore. We'll be praying for you."

Praying for her.

They'd buried children. They'd lost their boys and girls, a host of bright minds and inquisitive natures, and yet…

They were praying for her.

Hannah couldn't talk around the lump lodged in her throat, but she tried. "Thank you."

"No, Miss Moore. Thank you," Jill insisted. "And we'll be watching, hoping someday you can do the same things for other kids because you're special. And that's all we wanted to say. You have a good night now, okay?"

"Yes. Okay."

They disconnected the call with a shower of goodbyes, their encouraging voices food for her heart and soul.

"The righteous cry out and the Lord hears them…"

The sweet psalm's truth echoed in that phone call, an up-right blessing that strengthened Hannah's determination to do the best she could for her new students, facing forward, no matter what. *For when God is with us, who can stand against us?*

No one, Hannah decided, strength warming her heart. She

contemplated the phone, longing to call Jeff, but then decided against it, uncertain. A roomful of grief-stricken parents had just assuaged her soul with warmth and forgiveness. Jeff Brennan could learn a lot from their amazing example.

Hannah found two missed calls the next morning, both from Jeff, with a single cryptic message citing work constraints in place of church.

Hannah sighed, and headed to Holy Name, mixed feelings dogging her steps.

She longed to talk with him. Laugh with him. Spar with him.

But his exchange with Callie reaffirmed what she'd tucked aside. Jeff's romantic side came off as sweet and sincere, but she'd been fooled before.

Never again.

Hannah headed into the church, the grace of the Ironwood parents thrusting her forward.

Jeff Brennan was a player. He put work above all else and disavowed his brother, twin realities that said volumes more than sweet words.

Sure, he was nice to his grandma. And his sense of humor was a treasure she'd miss, that warm, frank smile and quick turn of phrase.

But an unforgiving nature left no foundation for building. Wasn't making amends part of life?

Her cell phone rang and Jane Dinsmore's name came up. "Jane, good morning. How are you?"

"I'm holding my own, dear, and I just wanted to congratulate you on a great beginning." Jane paused for breath, her fatigued voice underscoring her laborious fight. "Laura and Rose filled me in and just knowing you're there makes my physical struggles easier."

Her gentle words pricked Hannah's tears. "You focus on getting well. I'll hold down the fort in the meantime."

"And that's why I called, Hannah." Jane stopped again. Hannah waited, patient, allowing the older woman to catch her breath. "I'm putting in my retirement papers and I wanted you to be the first to know."

"But—"

"No buts. I may beat this thing and I'll be glad of it, but I've decided it's time to make a clean break. God has always appointed the paths in my life, and he's made this detour fairly obvious. I would love for you to stay on and apply for the full-time position, but that, of course, is up to you."

Her strength both humbled and inspired Hannah. "I would love to, Jane. Thank you."

A tiny laugh came through, a laugh that carried the hiccup of a sob before Jane disconnected the call. "No, honey. Thank you."

Hannah closed the phone, decisive. She'd head to the library, clean out her files and let Melissa know the job was about to be posted. Since the library was closed on Sunday, she could get her work done quickly and put things in motion for a new chapter in her life. Remembering Jeff's message, she longed for the whole brass ring, the fairy-tale happy ending, but if nothing else, she felt strong again. Ready to embrace life to the full.

She only wished that could have included Jeff Brennan.

Chapter Eighteen

Jeff watched the technician troubleshoot the factory's robotic application system, a machine crucial to on-time delivery of a current military contract. Quick glances to his watch intensified the loss of time, a day when he'd planned to see Hannah. Talk with her. See if he could set things straight.

"You got somewhere to be?"

The tech looked exaggeratedly at Jeff's watch. Jeff shook his head. "No, sorry, I just had things scheduled for today."

"Don't we all?" The tech resumed his position on the floor while adjustable work lamps flooded his area with light. "If it's shopping, go online. If it's family, I got nothin'."

Trent's foster father had reacted badly to his latest round of chemo. Trent had headed south, leaving Jeff on his own for a weekend that appeared worry free yesterday.

Today?

Jeff squared his shoulders, refusing to sigh, but hating having things not right with Hannah. Was she avoiding his calls deliberately?

His gut said yes, and that made talking to her imperative, but so was this work obligation. Jeff knew his job, he understood the consequences if supplies got held up in manufacturing. But right now he just wanted a few free hours to see his girl. Convince her he wasn't the conniver she thought him to be.

One look at the tech's face said that wasn't about to happen today.

Creak...

Hannah swung around, unable to identify the sound. She hadn't bothered turning all the library lights on, but foreboding clouds had deepened the gloom in the outer reaches of the library. Tall shelves blocked the little light the window offered, leaving her desk area lit while the rest of the room was dark. She checked the online forecast and sighed at the thought of more rain, but then it was November in the Alleghenies. Rain was a given.

Creeeaaak...

This time the noise drew her up straight, awareness crawling up her spine, tiny hairs rising in protest along her neck.

She saw nothing.

But she *felt* something, and she'd taught science long enough to understand the God-given gift of instinctive fear.

Why hadn't she locked the door? Why hadn't she turned on the lights?

Because this is Jamison, you ninny, her inner voice scolded. *You're letting your imagination run away with you. Turn on the lights, sip your coffee and finish up.*

She stood, crossed to the light panel inside the door and hit the bank of switches.

Dominic.

He stood framed in the back door, his hair messed up by the wind, his face haunted.

Hannah's heart seized. The clutch of surprise coupled with the dark skies, strong wind and the young man's angst transported her back in time to another place, another boy, another dark, stormy day.

Stay calm. Stay connected. Get to your cell phone.

She pulled in a breath, found it impossible to draw in fully with her chest constricted, and then worked to relax her gaze, her shoulders. "How did you get in? And why are you here?"

He came forward slowly, his eyes locked with hers, his look...

She'd seen that look before, she knew it well. Depression. Desolation. Desperation. The last time had preceded an out-of-control situation governed by a power-hungry gang of boys with no conscience, but this time...

Maybe this time she could help.

And then again...

Dominic withdrew a small handgun from the left-hand pocket of his trench coat as Hannah rethought her position. She held his gaze, nodded toward the gun and kept her voice firm with God's help. "Lose the gun, dude."

He shook his head, his jaw trembling.

Guide me, Lord. You wouldn't have brought me all this way, over all this time, without a reason. Give me strength. And wisdom. And please, please, please...keep me safe. Don't let me miss out on this new chance at a life renewed. Please.

She was near the door, but not close enough to escape, and she had no clue what Dominic intended. Did he want to hurt her? Hurt himself? Seeing the pain in his eyes, his face, she knew she couldn't turn away, but she wasn't willing to take foolish risks either. She thought of Jeff and regret stabbed her heart. Of Caitlyn, her little goddaughter, the niece she hadn't held yet.

But there was something about this boy that encouraged her to take a chance.

A big chance.

Making a decision, she moved toward her desk area and motioned him to come with her. "Sit down and tell me what's going on. But I don't talk to guns. If you want my help, lose the weapon. I mean it."

He stared at her for long ticks of the clock, then slid the gun back into his pocket.

Hannah sent him a disbelieving look. "Really?" She jerked her head toward the DVD drop box. "Put it in there, turn the lock and give me the key. Then we'll talk."

He paused, his indecision hiking her fears, but she absolutely refused to let dread govern this scene. She'd worked long and hard to retake her life, her destiny, and no way was she about to let anything mess that up. Or mess him up for that matter.

Although this kid had been raked over the coals already.

He headed for the lockbox, then darted a look over his shoulder as if expecting her to go for her cell phone or the library phone.

Hannah did neither; her inaction soothed the set of his jaw. *Good.*

He put the gun into the box, turned the key and tossed it to her. "You know I can get to it from outside, right?"

She nodded and shrugged. "But I know you won't. You didn't come here to hurt me, but you're thinking of hurting yourself and I won't stand for that in my library. Way too much cleanup. So sit." She motioned him to the chair alongside her and kept her face serene but strong. "And tell me what's going on. What's happened?"

"They're sending me away."

Of course they were. "Where?"

"Kessler Academy."

"Pricey."

He scowled. "Nothing but the best."

"Why?"

"Because they don't let you make choices at Kessler. If you're lagging in any area, they force you to take part, their sole goal being the production of young men of the highest quality, Ivy League–ready candidates."

"So if Penn or Princeton was your goal, you're all set. Tell me, Dominic." She put a hand on his arm after he sat down. "What are your goals?"

He dropped his head into his hands and grimaced. "I don't have goals. I just get by."

"Why?"

He looked up and frowned. "Because it's what I do."

"What you *choose* to do."

His frown deepened. "Well. Maybe."

"So choose differently."

"It's too late."

"Not as long as you're breathing, dude. What do you want out of life right now? As a teenager? And what do you want tomorrow? And next year? What do you see yourself doing, Dominic?"

"Designing."

Hannah paused, surprised.

Dominic pulled a handful of folded papers from his pocket. "I like to design things. My mother was an artist."

"Really?" Hannah opened the sheaf of papers and drew a breath, surprised by the depth and beauty of the commercial designs she held. "You did these? I mean, they're not some building you copied from seeing it online? Because, dude, these are gorgeous."

"You think?"

"Oh, Dominic, I know. Are the designs workable?"

The answer was there in the keen look of his eye, his quick nod. "That's the fun part of doing this, making sure the weight-bearing specs complement the beauty."

"Have you taken Computer-Aided Design?"

He shook his head. "My father won't let me. But Mr. Eschler and Mr. Bernard let me into the CAD lab when no one's around."

"They do, huh?" Hannah would have to rethink her assessment of the gnarly school custodian. It took a good heart to see the brilliant artist inside the angry child's body. "Do they have this option at Kessler?"

"No."

"Well, then." Hannah handed the speculative buildings and bridges back to him. "We need to talk to your father."

"My father doesn't listen. He talks. Then he walks away."

"Did you ever wonder why that is?" Hannah crept into this subject, not wanting to quench the light in Dominic's eyes.

"I know why. I remind him of my mother."

"And yet you look like your father." Hannah let the words dangle, then tapped the papers clutched in Dominic's hand. "Maybe *this* is what reminds him of your mother. Her talent, her artistry. And then you couple that with your anger and depression…" She sat back and let him absorb the idea, the suggestion that his behavior inspired his father's negative reactions. "Maybe your father is scared to death you'll do what your mother did, and doesn't know how to face that. Or change it."

The spark of recognition said her idea intrigued him so she continued. "Perhaps you can take charge of the situation by changing your actions, therefore inspiring different reactions from your father. Maybe you can find a common ground."

"Not with *her* around."

"Variables are a part of scientific exploration," Hannah reminded him. "Every researcher deals with the vagaries of the uncontrollable. But if your father is more content, your stepmother might be happier. Although I don't exactly see her as the happy-go-lucky type. You know that, don't you?"

A tiny smile quirked Dominic's mouth. "I get that."

"So…"

A police bullhorn interrupted their exchange.

Fear replaced Dominic's softened features, and Hannah knew she had two immediate tasks: to reestablish calm with Dominic because she had no idea what else he might have secreted in that coat, and to let the authorities outside know all was well.

He started to stand.

Hannah stopped him. "Stay low." She grabbed her cell phone. "Let me talk to them. I'll explain that we're fine, that all is well."

His stark terror belied her gentle words, but she held his hand while she dialed 911, hoping to stave off a weapons-drawn confrontation.

Hannah was in trouble. Big trouble.

Jeff raced to his car, Megan's worried voice hounding him. Why had he encouraged her to go back to teaching? Why didn't he put his foot down and condemn the foolish risk of his grandmother's plan? He'd seen the fear in Hannah's eyes, the stark reality of Ironwood imprinted on her face as she told her story.

He'd failed her by not taking her side, and now her well-being lay in the hands of a depressed teen with a gun, according to Megan.

Fear and anguish gripped his heart, his soul. Fear that something would happen before he could get to her, and angst that he didn't have sense enough to protect her. Put her first.

Protect her, God. Yes, I'm angry, we'll discuss that later, but please, please, please. Protect her. Guard her. Uphold her with Your righteousness, cradle her in the palm of Your hand. Please.

A blockade stopped him two blocks short of the library. The rain and wind drove the dark mood of the situation. The police had set up a command center at the convenience store on Route Nineteen. Jeff parked the car, barreled out and headed for the store.

"Hey. You. Back in the car, buddy, and head south. The road's closed."

Jeff raised his arms in the air. "My fiancée is in that library with the kid. I'm not going anywhere, Pete."

Pete Monroe peered closer, recognized Jeff and gave a quick nod. "Come with me."

He took Jeff into the store. What looked like commotion outside was well-organized within, but all Jeff heard was six words.

"We're in position."

"Then let's go."

He grabbed a detective's arm. "You're going in? When she's in there with a kid brandishing a gun? Are you crazy?"

An older man stood off to the side, his hands twining, his expression dark with terror.

The detective met Jeff's gaze with forced calm. "We're not going in, we're just announcing our presence. The blinds are drawn, we've got a tactical team coming so we can snake a camera in from the side vent. But they won't be here for a few minutes, and maybe the kid will negotiate."

"He's my son. He's got a name. It's Dominic," the father spouted from across the aisle. "Dominic Fantigrossi the third."

The detective nodded, his face grave. "I know that, Professor, and we're not trying to be insensitive. It's just a matter of working this out with no one getting hurt. Not Miss Moore." He directed his look to Jeff and Jeff read the concern in his eyes. "Or Dominic."

A part of Jeff wanted to ream out the older man, wondering just what a parent did to a kid to make him react this way, but another part remembered a boy whose father broke every civil and moral law known to mankind twenty years before...

He could have been a Dominic. For whatever reason, he chose to bury himself in work, striving to excel, but he remembered the embarrassment, the pain, the humiliation of being Neal Brennan's son.

Oh, yeah. He could have snapped back then and knowing

that was the only thing that kept him on his side of the room, away from the distraught father.

Protect her, please. Watch over her. And the kid. Please.

The detective's face darkened as he listened to whatever was being said through his earpiece, then he glanced Jeff's way, his jaw set. "We've made contact with Miss Moore. She wants to talk to you."

Jeff's heart leaped at this unexpected turn of events. "Have her call my cell."

The detective shook his head. "We've got to use ours for monitoring." He pointed to a communications setup beside the cash register. A cable snaked from the box to a van outside. Jeff moved closer just as the phone rang. He snatched it up, trying to disguise his fear. "Hannah?"

"Jeff. I need your help."

"Anything. You know that."

"Call them off."

Jeff surveyed the room full of cops and winced. "I can't, honey. Tell me your situation."

"I'm having a congenial meeting with a student. End of story."

"He's got a gun, Hannah."

"Not anymore, he doesn't. It's locked up in the DVD return box. And it isn't loaded. Never was. You tell the sheriff that what I've got is a scared kid and a teacher who isn't much better right now, having a normal conversation about teenage choices. If they lose the guns, they're welcome to come inside and see."

"You're okay? Really?"

"Really, truly." The strength in her voice said she was doing all right, considering. "You think I'm going to risk the future of my scarecrow, Jeff? Are you crazy?"

Her reference to the scarecrows sent him a solid message that she was fine, negotiating on her own, unforced.

"Have the police take the gun and stand down, then send

one calm guy in and we'll get Dominic home. He's scared, he's been depressed and no matter what happens, I'm not going to let anything happen to this kid, accidentally or self-induced. You got that, Dominic?" She'd obviously redirected her attention to the boy nearby, but kept her voice loud enough for Jeff's benefit. He heard the kid mutter an indistinct "yes."

Jeff gave the detective monitoring the call a thumbs-up.

The detective turned toward the professor. "You had no other guns in the house?"

"None." He shook his head, vehement. "That one was my father's, he left it to me. I don't use guns, I don't have bullets for it, even."

"And it's registered?"

"Yes."

The detective paused, inscrutable, then he contacted the officers surrounding the building. "I'm going in alone once we've secured the weapon. If everything's fine, I'll give the signal."

He didn't reiterate what would happen if everything wasn't all right, if Hannah had been coerced into making that call. But Jeff knew Hannah, her voice. She was mad, not scared. Nervous, not frightened. And frustrated that the situation had gone out of control.

But she was alive and talking, sounding wonderfully normal, and Jeff wanted nothing more than to keep it that way. When he started to follow the detective, a broad-shouldered deputy blocked his way. "Sorry. You've got to stay here."

"But—"

The deputy folded his arms and braced his legs, his face firm. "Let us do our job."

He was right, Jeff knew that, but he hated waiting in the wings.

Pray.

He paused, thought, accepted the cup of coffee the store clerk handed him and closed his eyes. *Keep her safe, Heavenly Father. Please. And, Lord, forgive me for getting her into this, for encouraging her, for letting my grandmother push her into a situation like this. Forgive us for stealing Your role, for messing with Hannah's life, her safety, her security.*

He could only imagine what she must have gone through, the terror, the flashbacks, the pain of reliving Ironwood.

And it was their fault for setting things in motion, encouraging her to get back into the classroom. None of this would have happened if she'd just been Hannah Moore, the Jamison librarian, quietly living her chosen life of obscurity.

Regret shaded his heart and soul. True love didn't take unnecessary risks or embrace harm. And yet he'd done just that, always striving to improve things. His mother, his life, his job, his company.

Was he ever satisfied with the status quo?

He'd have said yes regarding Hannah, but now he realized he'd tried to fix her, too. Right up to the point of endangering her life, her heart, her fragile psyche. What kind of a self-absorbed fool was he?

The worst, he realized as moments ticked on. Instead of trusting God to guide Hannah's path, he'd helped his grandmother direct her back into danger. And whatever price he had to pay for his know-it-all actions, so be it. Just as long as Hannah was all right.

Dear God in Heaven, please let Hannah be all right.

Chapter Nineteen

Hannah was going to go ballistic if someone didn't start listening to her. Dominic's face had paled with the initial police bullhorn announcement, and despite her best efforts to maintain calm, his nervousness was mounting.

She leaned in and held his gaze. "Look me in the eye and tell me you don't have any other weapons."

He shook his head. "Nothing. And I didn't even have bullets for the gun. I don't even know where to get bullets for that old gun."

"Good thing." Hannah paused, dropped her chin and uttered a prayer. "Dear God, we're in a situation here. Help the officers see we're okay, that everything's all right, that no one's going to get hurt. Keep everyone calm. Guide us. Shelter us. Protect us from harm."

Dominic arched a brow when she finished. "I thought teachers couldn't pray around students."

"Dude, do you *see* a school here?"

A little smile softened his face. "Good point."

"That's why I'm the teacher, you're the student. And if you get into trouble over this whole mess, I'll help you. But you've got to get hold of yourself. Depression and anxiety are not good soul mates. Try prayer. God. Church. Helping others. Put yourself out there, Dominic, and put others first. It's amazing how that realigns your perspectives."

"I can't believe you're talking this way when we have a SWAT team aiming guns at us."

Hannah waved that off, pretending nonchalance. "Jeff will set them straight. He knows when I'm doing all right and when I'm not."

"Since Ironwood?"

Hannah shifted a brow up. "You know about that?"

He nodded, sheepish. "I think that's why I came to you, because you'd understand. No one else seemed to. But since the day I saw you in the candy store, I kind of felt like you saw me. Knew me."

Hannah had felt exactly the same way. "We can thank the Holy Spirit for that one."

"You think God wants to help me?"

Hannah met his gaze. "God *is* helping you. He put us together, He gave us a chance to talk, to get to know one another. And He's probably given you other chances, Dominic, but you're too stubborn for your own good."

He didn't deny it. "I am."

"Which is where humility comes in. God blesses us in so many ways. Our job is to embrace and accept those ways. But first we have to recognize them."

"The glass being half-full."

"Exactly." A knock at the door drew Hannah to her feet. "I'm going to go let this officer in. I think you'd be smart to lie down, show them that you have no weapons and no ill intent, okay?"

Her instructions made him look fearful, but then he nodded and did as she asked. "Okay."

Hannah walked to the door and opened it. A lone officer stood outside, wet and bedraggled. She ushered him in, noting how he appraised the situation. Instead of handcuffing Dominic, he reached down and offered the kid a hand up.

"Dominic, I'm Detective Parsons of the Allegany sheriff's department. How are you doing?"

Dominic sent a look of surprise from the detective to Hannah. "Okay, I guess. Aren't you going to arrest me?"

"For?"

"Weapon possession?"

The detective gave him a benign look. "I don't see a weapon. Do you?"

"No, sir."

"And did you have ammunition for a weapon on your person today?"

"No, sir."

"And did you secure the unusable antique in a safe spot when asked?"

"Yes, sir."

"Well, then." The detective raised his hands. "I've got to do a pat down."

"Okay."

The detective ascertained that Dominic wasn't carrying anything else on his person, then checked his coat. "All clear." He stepped back and leveled a firm but kind look at Dominic. "Are you suicidal?"

Dominic paused, then shook his head. "No. I was upset, and wondering if the world might be better off without me before, but..." He shrugged and shifted his jaw toward Hannah. "I'm better now."

"And you, Miss Moore?"

"I'm fine. And Dominic knows he did the right thing by seeking help today, and the wrong thing by..."

"Taking my father's gun, loaded or not. I think I just wanted someone to take me seriously."

"You got your wish, kid." The detective passed a hand over his face, glanced up as though seeking divine inspiration, then keyed his mike. "We're good to stand down. Can you send the father and fiancé in here, please? With escort?"

"My father's here?" Dominic looked surprised and afraid, with good reason, Hannah supposed. And since Dominic Senior was married, the fiancé...

She could only hope they meant Jeff.

"Your father alerted us," the detective told Dominic. "He informed us that you and the gun were missing. He explained you were upset and possibly suicidal. When we realized you were here, alone with Miss Moore and she wasn't answering her phone..."

The door swung open. Dominic Senior entered first, his face wet, his color ashen. He grabbed his son in a hug and cradled the boy's head as if he might never let go.

"Hannah."

Hannah turned, overjoyed to hear Jeff's voice, see his face. He moved forward, studying her, his gaze raking her eyes, her cheeks, her mouth. He reached out and hugged her, then backed off and nodded, his voice level. "You're okay."

"Yes. Thank you for intervening for us."

He nodded, his expression unreadable, but she understood that. She'd brushed him off pretty thoroughly, refusing contact, ignoring his calls. No matter what happened, though, she'd always be grateful for his quick support today.

She turned toward the Fantigrossis and waved a hand toward the desk. "Can we talk?"

Dominic's father stared, wide-eyed. "Now?"

"Yes."

"After all this?" His arm indicated the detective, the scene outside, the weapon, his son.

"I think it's best." Hannah didn't dare look at Jeff just then. No way could she manage a professional meeting with a distraught parent and kid and an emotional one with Jeff at the same time.

In typical teacher fashion, she put the kid first and took a seat. Jeff moved off toward the children's section, removing himself from the situation. His cool distance broke her heart, but that had been her option, right? To ease away from his work-first mentality. Right now it felt like the worst choice she could have made, but…

She sat and motioned toward Dominic Senior. "Your son says you're sending him away."

The older man swallowed hard and nodded. "A prep school in Connecticut, yes."

"Because?"

The father frowned, then sighed. "Living with my wife and me is not easy for Dominic."

"Or you," Hannah suggested, keeping her voice easy.

"Any of us," the older man admitted. He met his son's gaze across the short expanse of space. "Your actions confuse me."

Young Dominic snorted. "They always did."

The older man shook his head and laid a hand on his son's arm. "That's not true. When you were little we had a lot of fun. You loved to go places with me, talk with me. But after your mother died—"

"You buried yourself in work and never came home."

The accusation pushed the older man back in his seat. He paused, thoughtful. "I did, yes. I buried myself because I couldn't face you and your grandparents, see the look that said if I'd been a better person, your mother would still be alive."

Young Dominic frowned. "It wasn't your fault. I knew that. Mom was different. Different from anyone."

"But—"

Dominic edged closer to his father. "There are no buts. Even as a kid I realized she was fragile. There were times when she was happy, but they didn't last long, and then she was just gone. And you were gone, and Grandma was so angry and every little thing I did was wrong."

A look of understanding brightened his father's features. "You didn't blame me?"

"No. I thought you stayed away because you blamed me,

that I wasn't good enough or smart enough. I mean, what kind of mother prefers death over her kid?" Young Dominic raised his shoulders in question.

"You had nothing to do with it," his father insisted. "She loved you, as much as she was able. It was life she hated. She couldn't handle things that came her way."

"I felt like it was my fault."

"I did, too."

The man and boy eyed one another, pondering the words. Dominic broke the silence first. "I can't go to Kessler. I won't. I'll go to counseling or therapy, and I'll join the science team if Miss Moore will still let me…." He flicked a look to Hannah, expectant.

"No guns?"

He flushed. "No. Sorry. That was stupid."

"No argument there." She glanced toward his pocket where a white corner indicated the sheaf of papers. "Do you have something to show your father, Dominic?"

Dominic sighed, withdrew the papers and handed them over. His father studied the drawings and the specs, an eyebrow upthrust, nodding as he went through them. "This is your work?"

"Yes."

"This is genius. Pure genius." He stared at his son, lofted the papers and surged forward, gathering Dominic into a hug. "This is amazing work. No one did these for you? These are yours?"

Dominic looked a little embarrassed, but quite pleased with the reaction his work inspired. "All mine. They're just sketches, Dad. Kind of rough at that."

"They're brilliant," his father reiterated, passing a hand across the structural image of a conjoined office complex. "You've combined your mother's talent for art and my head for science into something greater than both, and you don't even realize how special that is."

Young Dominic blushed. "It's not special. It's just me."

"It's beyond special," countered his father. He seized the boy and hugged him. "And you are amazing. I've been foolish to this point, Dominic, but I'm not foolish now. You'll stay home with us, I will go to therapy with you—"

Dominic drew back, surprised. "Really?"

"Yes. We're in this together and I should have realized how you felt long ago, but every time I saw the sadness in your eyes…"

"You thought of Mom."

His father acknowledged that, chagrined. "I did, yes."

Young Dominic pointed toward Hannah. "She told me that."

"Miss Moore." Dominic's father pulled Hannah into a hug. The younger man's surprise said his father wasn't much for spontaneous displays of affection. Dominic Senior stepped back, passed a hand across his face and gave her a watery smile. "Thank you. Thank you so much."

Hannah returned his look, fighting tears, but this time they were tears of joy. "You're welcome. And I do believe Dominic mentioned volunteer work at the church. Or perhaps with a charitable foundation in Wellsville?" She sent the teen an arch look. "There are lots of middle school kids who could use science tutors, as well."

He hugged her. "I will. Promise."

"And science team practice is every day at two-thirty, my classroom, ninety minutes. Be there."

"Yes."

He went out the door, the older man's arm slung around his shoulders, a poignant end to a rough day. The detective swept them a look, then faced Hannah. "Will they be okay?"

She nodded. "Yes."

He stuck out a hand. "You're some kind of woman, Miss Moore."

Her smile felt hollow. Jeff stood several feet away, his body language saying too much, and who could blame him? She was like that old cartoon character in the Sunday comics, the one that traipsed around with a dark cloud of doom over his head, a disaster waiting to happen.

Only today's disaster had been averted and she thanked God for that.

She turned to face Jeff as the detective headed for the exit. He studied her, his expression tight. "You're okay? Really?"

Except for the knot in her throat, she was fine. Just fine. "Yes."

"I can take you home."

She lifted her keys. "I've got my car."

"And you're okay to drive?"

"The whole four-minute drive?" She ignored his huff of breath and slipped into her jacket. "Yes."

She wasn't okay to do anything, not with his cool, stand-offish approach, but she'd been through this before and survived.

She'd get through it again.

A commotion at the door pulled her attention around. Jeff's brother, Matt, burst through, his worried expression sweeping the scene. "You're both all right?"

Jeff moved forward, reached out and clutched Matt's hand, the action surprising Hannah. "Yes, no thanks to me."

Matt shifted his attention from Jeff to Hannah and back. "Pete said you stayed calm and acted as liaison. I think that's pretty solid for a stuffed-shirt executive."

"That's decent praise from a blue-collar handyman."

Matt grinned and shifted his attention to Hannah. "You're really all right? Megan called Dana and Helen with a family alert."

Jeff grabbed his phone, but Matt stopped him. "I called, told them everything was fine. Of course they'll want to see for themselves so you better stop over there. Let them get a look at the hero."

"I'm no hero." Jeff turned and faced Hannah, determined to have his say, wishing she didn't look so sweet, so endearing. "I should never have encouraged you to go back to teaching. Or let my grandmother push you."

Hannah frowned. "You didn't."

Jeff wasn't about to take the easy way out. "I did, because I thought it would be good for you, but now…" He waved a hand around, indicating the library. "After all this…" He paused, sucked in a breath and shrugged. "I'm sorry, Han. So sorry."

Matt stepped back, his hands up. "Private stuff. I get it." He turned Jeff's way. "If the offer to bunk at your place still holds, I could use a decent night's sleep. The bank emailed me that the closing is tomorrow, and I'd like to have a working brain."

Jeff withdrew his key ring and tossed Matt the house key. "Make yourself at home."

"You've made up?" Hannah eyed both men, then turned her attention to Jeff. "You're being nice to your brother?"

He shrugged, hating to make a big deal out of something he should have done long ago. "Family first, right?"

Hannah's smile bloomed. "Yes. Always."

Matt headed toward the door. "See you guys."

Jeff barely noticed, Hannah's smile drawing him closer. "I called you."

She winced. "I know."

"You were avoiding me."

The wince turned into a grimace. "Yes. When I saw you with Callie, and knew you weren't being honest with her…" Her voice trailed off. She shrugged.

Jeff wanted to move closer, but he needed to say this, clear the air. "You assumed I was guilty and shut me out."

She had, but for good reason, right?

One look at Jeff's face said no. "You were feeding Callie a line. We both know that."

Jeff shook his head. "I was *walking* a thin line, yes, because I promised Matt to keep his deal confidential and I'd almost ruined it once. To make amends to my brother, I needed to honor his wishes."

"His deal?" Hannah frowned, not understanding.

"Matt's about to close on Callie's father's subdivision." *Cobbled Creek.*

Hannah sighed, chagrined.

"So when I apologized to Matt and promised to stay out of his way—"

"And offered him a place to bunk…"

"Yes. I couldn't exactly be forthright with Callie because the deal is out of our hands and I didn't want to betray Matt." This time he moved closer, his gaze saying something else. Something more. "But mostly I hated to see that disappointment in your eyes."

And that was exactly how she'd felt that night, as if her knight in shining armor fell way short of his horse. She took a step forward, halving their distance. "I'm sorry. I shouldn't have doubted you."

Jeff closed the last little bit of distance, reached out and tipped her chin up. "Faith, hope and love."

She wrinkled her brow.

"From this moment forward I want you to have faith in me and know it's well deserved."

The thought of trusting him seemed amazingly right. "That sounds doable."

He slipped one arm around her waist, drawing her in. "And I want to inspire hope in you, every single day. Hope for today and hope for tomorrow."

Gentle words. Inspirational words. She tilted her head, wanting more. "And love?"

He smiled down at her, his gaze a promise. "That one's easy. I love you, Hannah, and I'll spend every day showing you that if you'll let me. Be my wife. Have my babies. Deal with the sometimes crazy demands of my job. Can you do that, Han?" He swept her lips a gentle kiss that stretched into something deeper, more meaningful as long seconds ticked by. When he finally broke the kiss, he cradled her face between two strong hands, his gaze sincere. "Can you handle the way my job pulls me sometimes, because it's not likely to change."

She met his gaze, leaned up and kissed him back. "Neither is mine, Jeff, so I'll ask you the same thing. Can you handle knowing that I'll be in that classroom day after day? And that sometimes you'll be on diaper duty because I'm doing test prep or science team practice?"

He laughed and hugged her close. "That's what grandmas are for, honey. Haven't you heard?"

The idea of Dana and Helen helping with their future children didn't sound bad at all. "That sounds like some good strategic planning to me."

"Me, too." Jeff settled one more sweet, long kiss to her mouth, then dropped to one knee. "I believe there's a proper way to finalize this deal."

She smiled through watery eyes.

"Will you marry me? Be my wife? Deal with a stuffed-shirt corporate exec for the rest of your days?"

Nothing on God's green earth could make her happier. "Yes. And soon, please. I want to be your wife, savor every moment God gives us."

Jeff grinned, rose and gave her one last kiss before they headed out the door. The rain had gentled to a cool mist, a welcome respite from the earlier torrent. "Then I suggest we head to my mother's, prove we're fine and make her day by letting her take over the details."

Hannah squeezed his hand. "That's perfect, Jeff."

"Of course it is." He grinned, cocky and delightfully self-assured, but also sincere. "And then the scarecrows can move in together and live happily ever after."

Hannah beamed up at him. "That will make Mrs. Scarecrow very happy."

His answering grin said Mrs. Scarecrow wouldn't be the only one. Hannah blushed and ducked into her car. "I'll follow you, okay?"

He leaned in, gave her one last kiss and stepped back, his smile a blessing. "I couldn't ask for anything more, Hannah."

Epilogue

"We don't have to go," Jeff told Hannah the following Fourth of July, his expression reflecting his concern. Having glimpsed her face in the mirror, she didn't have to ask why, but...

No way was she about to stay home.

"Of course we have to go," she told him, grabbing her bag and breathing slowly, hoping the maneuver worked. Sometimes it did, and sometimes, well... "It's the ribbon-cutting ceremony for the Farmers Free Library, the project that—" she stepped closer to him and swiped a gentle hand across the furrowed lines of his brow "—brought us together. We're not going to let a little thing like morning sickness keep us from it."

"Are you sure?" He cupped her cheek with his palm, his gaze intent. "I could go and send your apologies. Everyone would understand."

"Or I can go and stay far away from anything that smells like cooking meat, which shouldn't be a problem this morning. But the Independence Day Festival later..."

"We'll take a pass on," Jeff announced. "You've got your crackers?"

She patted her bag.

"Ginger ale?"

"In the car."

"All right." He grasped her hand as they headed outside, then gently nudged her as they crossed the broad front porch. "You know people talk about us, don't you?"

"As well they should," she quipped, pretending she didn't understand. "We're young, reasonably good-looking professionals, newly married and expecting our first child before the end of the year. We've given them a lot of things to consider."

"I meant them." Jeff pointed to the porch where a family of scarecrows made a cheerful appearance, their broomstick ends thrust into fresh bales of straw. "Shouldn't we put them away until fall?"

Hannah didn't have to feign surprise. "They're dressed appropriately, Jeff. I've seen to that. And I like seeing them there, all cute and funny in their cutoffs and tank tops. That little red-haired boy scarecrow is adorable, isn't he? Do you have any redheads in your family? Because I don't, but I always thought it would be fun to have a red-haired child."

"People think we're weird because scarecrows are a traditional fall decoration."

"People are silly. Farmers use scarecrows all summer long. Why can't we?"

He could have given a laundry list of reasons, but Jeff had learned the valued lesson of picking battles. With Hannah's morning sickness making these last couple of weeks distinctly uncomfortable, he'd let the scarecrow issue slide. He knew their summer garb only made the straw family seem like a bigger oddity to passersby, but if it made Hannah happy…

He sighed, patted her knee and pulled out of the drive, figuring the straw family could become permanent inhabitants as long as Hannah was happy.

They pulled into the already crowded grass lot several minutes later, the early July sun intense despite the morning hour.

"Over here, you two!" Cindy Pendleton, his grandmother's no-nonsense secretary, directed them to the front of the library where a big red, white and blue ribbon marked the holiday and the ceremonial reopening. "We need to get pictures for the paper and you guys are late." One look at Hannah's face had Cindy shrugging an arm of comfort around Hannah's waist. "It gets better, I promise. Usually," she added with her typical candor. "How far along are you?"

"Sixteen weeks."

Cindy nodded. "It should ease up soon. I can't begin to tell you how excited your grandmother is. She's beside herself. Instead of work specs on her desk, I find baby catalogs. Online receipts for the myriad of things she's already ordered."

"She's adorable."

"Mmm-hmm." Cindy sent Hannah a dubious look. "When all this stuff ends up at your door, remember that. I keep reminding her that babies really need two things—a mother and diapers—but she won't hear a thing I'm saying."

"Then I'm glad we've got a four-bedroom house," Jeff cut in. "And storage over the garage."

Cindy placed them strategically with the rest of the fundraising committee and the local newspaper photographer snapped several pictures. Then they lined up Helen, Jeff and Hannah to do the ribbon cutting. "Jeff, you do it," Helen insisted. "Hannah and I will flank you."

"Nope." He put the wide scissors into Hannah's hand and stepped aside. "You two do it together. If I'd had my way I wouldn't have been involved in any of this, and it's only your tenacity—" he sent a direct look to his grandmother "—and your courage—" he switched his gaze to his wife "—that got us here. So, ladies, smile for the camera…." They did, Hannah and Helen grasping the scissors together as a local news crew caught the breaking ribbon on camera. "Let's open the doors so people can examine the fruits of their labors."

Clean red brick had replaced worn vinyl siding. The library had nearly tripled in size, and while still small, it now housed the technology of big-city branches on a more minute scale. They moved inside; the new air-conditioning was a delightful respite from the summer sun. Cool drinks and coffee waited in the social room, a gathering spot in the new wing to the west of the building, the entire room paid for by a significant donation from the Fantigrossi family.

And at that very moment, both Dominics strode into the new facility. The professor pumped a few hands on the way, but young Dominic headed straight for Hannah. "Did you read my applications?"

She nodded. "Of course. They were fine, nothing less than I'd expect. And I like how you used your troubled times as your essay in two of them. It makes you sound real and college boards like kids who don't sound manufactured. I added my recommendation letters to each of them."

He grimaced, then smiled. "I was *too* real for a while, that's for sure. But things are better now."

"And your father's doing okay?"

Dominic nodded. "It's been rough since my stepmother left, but yeah. He's doing all right."

"And you?"

He pumped out a breath, glanced around and gave her a firm nod. "I feel normal. I mean, I *think* I feel normal, but it took so long that I'm not even sure what normal is anymore. But I'm definitely doing better."

Hannah had no trouble relating. "I understand completely."

He smiled and it softened his young features. "I knew you would."

A commotion at the door drew their attention. Hannah moved forward as Trent Michaels wheeled Jane Dinsmore into the foyer. Her look of delight downplayed the gravity of her condition. A wig covered the aftereffects of her latest round of chemo. She beamed as Hannah and Jeff approached, then clasped Hannah's hands in hers in a gesture of respect and honor. "I've heard your good news, and while I'm quite fond of babies in the abstract having raised none of my own, I'm hoping you're modern enough to want to teach *and* have a family." She squeezed Hannah's hands lightly. "The proper response to that is a simple *yes*."

Hannah laughed and kissed the older woman's cheek. "Yes. We've got day care all lined up and since my schedule will coincide with the kids' schedules once they get older, it would be silly to stop doing what I love. As a teacher, I get the best of both worlds. A great profession and time with my kids."

"I'm so glad, Hannah. And I wish I'd been here to see that first-place win in the state science championship," Jane added.

Hannah waved toward young Dominic who was now stuffing his face full of cheese and crackers, looking wonderfully normal for a seventeen-year-old. "Dominic shored up our weak physics link. After that, it was a walk in the park."

Jane's smile said she knew better, but she nodded toward Hannah's midsection. "Do we know if it's a boy or girl yet? And have you picked names?"

"Too early to know," Jeff explained. He slipped an arm around Hannah's waist, letting her take the second question.

"If it's a boy, we're going to name him Jonas, after his great-grandfather."

"Lovely." Jane beamed and nodded. "Helen will be so pleased. And if it's a girl?"

Hannah exchanged a smile with Jeff and bent closer. "We'll call her Jane, after you, and we can only hope she'll grow up to be the kind of woman she's named for. Jane Alice Brennan."

Quick tears filled Jane's eyes. "I don't know what to say. I'm overwhelmed."

"Say you'll keep up the good fight so you can be around to see your namesake," Jeff told her. "If it's a girl, of course."

"I will." She nodded, vigorous, dabbing at her eyes with the tissue Hannah provided. "And if it's a boy, I'll just stay healthy enough until we have a girl."

Hannah crouched to Jane's wheelchair level, her smile forthright. "Your job is to get better and see what happens, because this is one experiment we have no control over."

"So we let go and let God," Jane offered, determined.

Hannah felt the warmth of Jeff's hand on her shoulder, the grace of new life within and the scope of opportunities she'd embraced by being pushed out of her comfort zone less than a year before. She smiled, her heart full, her soul content. "Amen."

* * * * *

Dear Reader,

My son-in-law did a youth ministry stint in Littleton, Colorado. A local host family took him to see Columbine High School, the scene of a heinous attack. Jon's guide told him "Most of the teachers that were here have gone." That single sentence sent my brain spinning.

Where did they go? What shadows followed them? How do you deal with a conscienceless act that happens on your watch?

And so began *Mended Hearts,* the story of a survivor who regains her hold on normalcy and the man who reminds her of her past. It's a story of redemptive strength, of gathering scattered pieces and realizing Humpty Dumpty *can* be fixed. It just takes faith, hope, love and time.

Our family has four wonderful high school teachers. I worked for nine years in a segregated classroom with angry middle school kids. Many bore little conscience. My poverty-stricken youth taught me that good teachers *do* make a difference. Their impact resounds long after that last bell rings. And true teachers are born to teach, intrinsic to their heart and soul.

I hope you love this story of regaining strength and mustering faith, of bold steps forward in the sweet setting of Allegany County, NY, one of God's prettiest places. I love to hear from readers. Your words bless me. Visit me and "the guys" online at www.menofalleganycounty.com or come play with me at "Ruthy's Place," www.ruthysplace.com, where I shamelessly exploit cute kids, pets and recipes because it's, well…fun. You can email me at ruthy@ruthloganherne.com or snail mail me c/o Love Inspired Books, Harlequin Enterprises, 233 Broadway, Suite 1001, New York, NY 10279.

God bless you and keep you!

Ruthy

QUESTIONS FOR DISCUSSION

1. Matt's sudden reappearance in town angers Jeff. We realize that Jeff has unresolved feelings regarding his half brother. Does pushing our feelings aside help us heal? Or do they just ferment over time?

2. Hannah assumes she is thrust into the library fundraising project because of her job. Later we find out that Helen knew who she was and timed the fundraising for when Hannah was strong enough to handle it. Has the Holy Spirit ever "organized" things in your life, waiting until just the right time for circumstances to nudge you forward?

3. Jeff reminds Hannah of Brian, her former fiancé. Reminders of Brian inspire memories of Ironwood High, the two traumas interconnected. How difficult is it to handle trauma in our lives? And how does faith help us to heal?

4. In an act of self-protection, Hannah works small jobs to keep from becoming invested. Despite that, she's fallen in love with Allegany County. Her attraction to Jeff could endanger that. What if things don't work out? Her fears make it difficult to take chances. Have you ever been afraid to step out? How did you conquer that fear?

5. Hannah's brother and sister-in-law give birth to a baby girl. Caitlyn's birth reminds Hannah that life goes on and gives her a forward thrust. She realizes fear is not of God and decides to consciously work to conquer it. Has taking a firm step forward ever helped you heal?

6. Matt Cavanaugh says he's come back to Wellsville and Jamison to work, but he's also there to make amends and atone for his youthful sins. How hard would it be to go back and face those you hurt?

7. Jeff's mother and grandmother cut him no slack regarding his attitude toward Matt. They see Matt as another victim of Neal Brennan's callous disregard for others. Their inclusion of Matt angers Jeff. He thinks his self-righteous anger is understandable, but God nudges him forward, forcing him to see the whole picture. Have you ever clung to anger like Jeff? How did you let it go and move on?

8. Jane Dinsmore's illness is the catapult Hannah needs to face her bigger fear: returning to the classroom. Once there, she realizes the anticipation was worse than the deed. How often have you let worry consume you, only to realize the reality isn't all that bad?

9. Hannah reveals her past to Jeff while she contemplates returning to the classroom. Jeff's feelings are torn, but he wants what's best for her. When Hannah's safety is threatened by an angry student, Jeff feels as if he let her down. How difficult is it to know which way to go, what choices to make? And have you ever given advice that backfired? How did you fix that?

10. Hearing what Hannah endured at Ironwood shames Jeff. He sees his resentment of Matt through grown-up eyes finally. He seeks Matt out and apologizes and offers assurance that they're family and family sticks together. Have you ever had to admit you were wrong and openly swallow your pride? Humble yourself? Was it difficult to do?

11. Dominic is an example of a lost soul in a dysfunctional family. How important is it for families to talk things out? Share their feelings? Share their faith? How did Dominic's father allow guilt to separate him from his son?

12. Christ promised life to the full, but God entrusted man with free will. When evil arises, how hard is it to regain that promised life? How can we help others who've experienced a grievous loss?

INSPIRATIONAL

Inspirational romances to warm your heart & soul.

TITLES AVAILABLE NEXT MONTH

Available September 27, 2011

THE CHRISTMAS CHILD
Redemption River
Linda Goodnight

THE COWBOY'S LADY
Rocky Mountain Heirs
Carolyne Aarsen

ANNA'S GIFT
Hannah's Daughters
Emma Miller

BUILDING A FAMILY
New Friends Street
Lyn Cote

HEALING AUTUMN'S HEART
Renee Andrews

OKLAHOMA REUNION
Tina Radcliffe

REQUEST YOUR FREE BOOKS!

2 FREE INSPIRATIONAL NOVELS
PLUS 2
FREE
MYSTERY GIFTS

Love Inspired®

Love Inspired

Cody Jameson knows that hiring gourmet chef Vivienne Clayton to cook for the Circle C Ranch *has* to be a mistake. Back in town for just a year, Vivienne wonders how she'll survive this place she couldn't wait to leave. To everyone's surprise, this big-city chef might actually stand a chance of becoming a cowboy's lady forever.

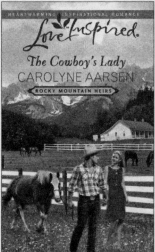

The Cowboy's Lady
by Carolyne Aarsen